'I used to think some dreams and wishes would come true if I wished and dreamed hard enough, but they never did.'

'What did you wish for?' he asked after a short pause.

Erin crossed her arms over her chest—not so much because of the chill of the autumn air, but more to control the pain she felt deep inside her chest. 'I don't know…just things…'

She looked down and Bridget the dog came back over to where they were standing, her plumy tail wagging softly. Eamon bent down and ruffled her ears. 'Maybe it's all about timing,' he said, straightening. 'When the planets are aligned maybe your dreams will come true.'

Erin looked at him again. 'So you're a romantic, Dr Chapman, are you?'

His gaze went to her mouth. 'You'd better believe it, Dr Taylor,' he said, and covered her mouth with his.

Dear Reader

One of the most rewarding aspects of being a globally published author is the opportunity it gives me to raise awareness of certain issues that are very dear to me. By purchasing this book you are actively helping me help The Australian Childhood Foundation in their quest to stamp out child abuse and neglect in Australia. I will be donating all my proceeds from this book to the Foundation, and hope that in doing so many children's lives will be changed for the better.

It has been said that every childhood lasts a lifetime. The memories some children carry from their childhood are not ones any child should be burdened with. Please join me in helping this great cause as it works to educate and advocate for children who have no one else to fight for them.

With best wishes

Melanie Milburne

EMERGENCY DOCTOR AND CINDERELLA

BY
MELANIE MILBURNE

Melanie Milburne says: 'One of the greatest joys of being a writer is the process of falling in love with the characters and then watching as they fall in love with each other. I am an absolutely hopeless romantic. I fell in love with my husband on our second date, and we even had a secret engagement, so you see it must have been destined for me to be a Harlequin® Mills & Boon author! The other great joy of being a romance writer is hearing from readers. You can hear all about the other things I do when I'm not writing, and even drop me a line at: www.melaniemilburne.com.au'

Praise for
Melanie Milburne:

Melanie Milburne also writes for Modern™ Romance!

I dedicate this book to Joe Tucci and Dani Colvin,
who first approached me to be an ambassador
for the Australian Childhood Foundation—
a position I accepted with great enthusiasm.

CHAPTER ONE

IT WAS the third day in a row that someone had parked in Erin's spot. Not only had they parked there arrogantly, they had done so crookedly, taking up so much space she had to manoeuvre her car into the space near the garbage-disposal unit, which she knew would almost certainly result in a scratch or two on her shiny paintwork.

She rummaged in her handbag for a piece of paper and a pen, and then, glancing around for a flat surface, whooshed out a breath and leaned on the rogue-parker's bonnet to pen her missive: *you are in the wrong spot!*

Erin tucked the note behind one of the windscreen wipers and made her way to the elevator. She tapped her right foot impatiently as she watched the numbers light up as it came down from the fifteenth floor. After a ten-hour shift in the emergency department of Sydney Metropolitan, the only thing she wanted was the quiet, safe sanctuary of her apartment. Her ears were still ringing from the shattered cries of a middle-aged mother who had lost her only son to a fatal stab-wound—yet another drug deal gone wrong.

The doors of the elevator glided open and she came face to face with a tall man who was wearing blue denim jeans and a white T-shirt that had a dust smear over the right shoulder. He was carrying an empty cardboard box and he smiled at her crookedly as he stepped out. 'Moving in,' he explained with a flash of perfect white teeth.

Erin lifted her chin and gave him a gimlet glare. 'Is that your car in my parking space?'

Something hardened in his green gaze and his smile flatlined. 'I was not aware there were designated parking spaces.'

Her chin went a little higher. 'The numbers are painted on the ground. A blind man could see them.'

One of his dark brows lifted along with his top lip, as if controlled by the same muscle. 'You must be the woman from 1503,' he said, rocking back on his heels slightly. 'I was warned about you.'

Erin felt her hackles rise like the fur of a cornered cat. 'I beg your pardon?'

His eyes moved over her rigid form with indolent ease. 'Erin Taylor, right?'

She tightened her mouth. 'That's correct.'

He smiled a smile that was borderline mocking. 'My landlord told me all about you.'

'Oh, really?' She affected a bored, uninterested tone.

'Yes,' he said, placing the box on the concrete floor. 'You're a doctor at Sydney Metropolitan.'

Erin mentally rolled her eyes. *Here comes another free car-park consultation*, she thought. No doubt he thought he could weasel a flu shot out of her, like one of her neighbours had tried to do as soon as autumn had kicked in last month. 'Yes, that's right,' she said crisply. 'And right now I am off duty, so if you'll excuse me?'

'I'm renting the apartment next to yours,' he said.

'How…er…nice,' Erin said with no attempt to sound sincere.

The man's lazy smile travelled all the way up to his green eyes, making them crinkle up at the corners. 'I guess in the interests of neighbourly peace I should move my car.'

'You should,' she said, stabbing at the call button to reopen the doors. 'But don't use the disabled spot. Mrs Greenaway on level ten uses that.'

'I'll try and remember that.'

Something about his tone made Erin feel as if he was laughing at her behind his urbane smile. She gave the call button an even harder jab, trying not to notice how his T-shirt clung to his lean but muscular frame. She had seen a lot of male bodies over the years so it took a particularly good one to make her do a double-take. This one was seriously fit. No spare flesh, just hard, toned muscle on a six-foot-three, maybe six-foot-four-inch frame. His hair was a rich, dark brown, several shades darker than hers, and his skin was the sort that tanned easily. His twelve-plus-hours-since-he'd-last-shaved stubbled jaw had a hint of stubbornness to it, and his blade of a nose, teamed with those penetrating green eyes, gave him a 'take no prisoners' air that she found strangely compelling.

The elevator doors pinged open, and Erin stepped in and pressed the button for the fifteenth floor. For the sake of common politeness, she forced her lips into a non-committal smile that didn't quite make the distance to her eyes. 'See you around,' she said.

'Yeah, no doubt you will.' He smiled an inscrutable little smile in return.

The elevator doors closed and Erin let out the breath

she hadn't even realised she had been holding. She gave herself a mental shake. The tall, dark, handsome neighbour was certainly a welcome change from the previous tenants: a trio of university students who'd partied non-stop and who, to add insult to injury, had put their rubbish in Erin's bin when theirs had been full. It had taken the last two weeks to get the smell of cigarette smoke out of her curtains, since the apartments were linked by a common balcony with only a waist-height glass partition to separate them.

As long as the new tenant stayed out of her way and out of her parking space, Erin was sure they would get along just fine.

'Morning, Erin.' Tammy McNeil, the triage nurse on duty in A&E, greeted Erin the next morning. 'How come you didn't come to the new director's breakfast meeting? He insisted all the A&E doctors on duty today attend. He wants to meet everyone in person, even the cleaning staff.'

Erin placed her bag in the locker under the desk before she straightened to answer. 'I had better things to do—like catch up on some much-needed sleep. I'm sure we'll cross paths sooner or later.'

Tammy perched on the corner of the desk. 'You don't look like you had such a great night's sleep. I know yesterday's death was rough on you. The mum was a bit over-the-top trying to blame you for not saving her son. Are you OK? You look exhausted.'

Erin hated it when people told her she looked tired; it made her feel tired even when she wasn't—although last night had been a rough one, she had to admit, even without the drama of the young man's death. Right until the early hours, she had heard furniture and boxes being dragged across the floors next door, and even though she had put a pillow over her head it hadn't really helped, for when she had finally drifted off to sleep she had woken several times in an agitated state from some vivid nightmares. It always happened after she had to deal with drug-affected patients. The ghosts from the past haunted her when she was most vulnerable. 'I'm fine, Tammy,' she said, reaching for her stethoscope. 'I'm used to patients and their relatives using me as a scapegoat. It's part of the job. It's not as if I have to ever see them again. That's one of the benefits of working as an A&E doctor: I treat them as best I can and then I leave them to someone else to follow up.'

Tammy gave her a wry look as she hopped down off the desk. 'Mmm, well, you might have to have a rethink about that after you hear about Dr Chapman's plan for the department.'

Erin shrugged herself into her white coat, pulling her hair out from beneath the collar and tying it back in a neat bun with an elastic tie she had in her coat pocket. 'I don't care what Dr Chapman has planned for the department. He can't make me work any harder than I do.' She picked up her name-badge and clipped it to her coat. 'If he's anything like our previous director, he'll realise we're all doing the best we can and leave us to get on with it.'

Tammy winced. 'Er...'

Erin frowned at her. 'What's the matter?'

A deep, clipped voice spoke from behind Erin. 'Dr Taylor—a word, please. In my office. Now.'

Erin turned, her eyes widening when she saw the man from the elevator standing there. 'I'm about to start my shift,' she said. 'There are five bays already occupied, waiting for assessment.'

His green eyes were like steel darts pinning hers. 'There are two other doctors and a registrar on duty. I am sure they are well able to cope without you for five or ten minutes.'

Erin pulled her mouth into a resentful line as she followed him out of the department to the office he had been allocated next to X-ray. He held open the door for her and she swept past him, bristling with irritation.

He closed the door and strode over to his desk, which was in a state of moving-in disarray. 'Please take a seat,' he said. 'I won't keep you long.'

Erin hesitated for a brief moment. If she sat down it would give him an advantage she didn't want him to have. He was so tall, standing there looking down at her, making her feel about fifteen years old when she was nearly twice that age. His hard gaze tussled with hers, and she sat like a heavy bag of theatre laundry being dropped. She folded her arms across her chest and swung one leg across the other, in a 'let's get this over with' pose that she knew reeked of insolence, but she was beyond caring.

'Perhaps I should introduce myself properly since I neglected to do so last night,' he said.

'Why didn't you?' she asked with a curl of her top lip. 'You clearly knew who I was given you were "warned" about me.'

Eamon decided against taking the chair behind his desk. Instead he leaned back against the filing cabinet and surveyed Erin Taylor's pursed lips and flashing, chocolate-brown eyes. She was sitting in a combative pose, every feminine inch of her poised to strike. He decided she would be quite astonishingly beautiful if she would smile instead of scowl. She had clear skin with just a dusting of light brown freckles over her uptilted nose. Her chestnut hair was glossy, and even though she had arranged it into a tight chignon at the back of her head a few escaping wisps framed her heart-shaped face. Her mouth was full, although it was currently pulled tight, and her cheekbones were classic, like a model's, sharp and high with a hint of haughtiness about them. Her body was slight but unmistakably feminine; her breasts were pushed up by her tightly crossed arms, giving him a clear view of her cleavage, which he was almost certain was unintentional.

He felt a stirring in his groin which took him completely by surprise. Admittedly it had been a while since he had held a woman in his arms, but somehow he couldn't see Erin Taylor falling into his bed any time soon—although in his head he rubbed at his jaw; there was nothing he liked more than a tough challenge.

'As you already know, I am Dr Eamon Chapman, the new A&E director,' he said. 'You would have received the email about my appointment.'

She didn't answer; she just sat there staring at him with that recalcitrant look on her face.

'You would have also received the invitation to a breakfast meeting this morning which apparently you decided against attending,' he continued.

She sat up even straighter in her chair. 'It wasn't compulsory.'

Eamon pushed his tongue into his right cheek as he fought to keep cool. Something about her reminded him of a defiant schoolgirl with little or no respect for authority. 'No,' he said. 'But it would have been polite to inform me you were unable to attend. As you can imagine, this position is a busy and highly demanding one. I would appreciate every member of the team I am directing to be one-hundred-percent committed from day one of my appointment. That includes you, Dr Taylor.'

Erin raised her chin. 'I worked a ten-hour shift yesterday and a twelve-hour the day before,' she said stiffly. 'I give one hundred and twenty percent to this place.'

'All the more reason for you to be aware of my plans to improve the department,' he said with equal tension.

Erin felt like rolling her eyes. How many times had some bureaucrat come in with a hot-shot plan to revamp the place? It didn't matter what fancy plans Dr Chapman had drawn up; within a few months it would be back to double shifts, patients lying in the corridors and ambulances lined up in the street due to the lack of beds. 'OK, then,' she said, giving him a cynical look. 'Why don't you fill me in now so I'm all up to date?'

He pushed himself away from the filing cabinet and picked up a document from his desk. 'It's all in here,' he said, handing it to her. 'Perhaps you'll do me the honour of reading it at your leisure and getting back to me with any questions or suggestions.'

Erin took the document but in the process of doing so encountered his long, tanned fingers for a fraction of a second. It felt like a lightning bolt had zapped up her arm at the brief contact. She tried her best to cover her reaction by casually flipping through the twenty-page document, but the words, although neatly typed, made no sense at all to her. It was as if her brain had shut down. Her body felt hot and tight, as if her skin had shrunk two sizes on her frame. She could feel her face heating under his silent scrutiny, and she shifted uncomfortably in her chair. The air she breathed in contained a hint of his aftershave; it was lemony and fresh, not cloying or overpowering like some she had smelt.

She heard him shuffle through some papers on his desk and looked up to encounter his emerald gaze trained on her. 'There is another matter I wish to discuss with you,' he said. 'I understand a patient died in A&E yesterday.'

Erin hardly realised she had moved but she suddenly found herself sitting on the edge of her chair. 'Yes, that's correct,' she said. 'He'd virtually bled out by the time he arrived here—he was in grade-four shock and went into asystole. I did his resus by the book.'

'I'm sure you did, Dr Taylor,' he said. 'But a formal complaint has been made by a relative, and as director I am responsible for seeing that it is investigated thoroughly.'

Erin felt her spine give a nervous wobble that travelled all the way down her legs. 'That resus was textbook EMST, Dr Chapman. I've documented the whole episode, and you can watch it on the CCTV as well,' she said, forcing her voice to remain composed and confident.

'The mother of the young man who died...' He glanced at the paper before pinning Erin with his gaze once more. 'The resus might have been technically correct, when it occurred, but what about its timing? Mrs Haddad maintains that you did not respond quickly enough to her son's injuries. She said that they were waiting in A&E for more than an hour before he was properly assessed.'

Erin drew in a scalding breath. 'That is not true! The triage nurse informed me of his injuries and I went straight to him from an asthmatic I was treating. The boy had multiple abdominal stab-wounds and was in hypovolemic shock. I was told that and went straight to the resus bay. I would have seen him within a couple of minutes at most after he arrived. If he was waiting around for treatment, it certainly wasn't here. Maybe they were hanging about in the waiting room, or outside the department. All I know is that as soon as I was told of his arrival I finished injecting prednisolone to a severe asthmatic, made sure she was inhaling the ventolin nebuliser and supervised by a nurse, and went straight to the resus bay. Three minutes at most.'

Eamon Chapman didn't speak but continued to look at her with that piercing green gaze of his.

'You know what some relatives can be like,' Erin argued. 'They don't believe their loved one was involved in something shady. "He's a good boy" and all that. "Someone else did this to him". "The doctors didn't save him". Blame anyone and everyone except the person responsible.'

Eamon put the paper back down on his desk. 'I realise emotions run high in cases like this for everyone involved. Mrs Haddad may well withdraw the complaint after legal counsel. But even so there are still some issues that need to be dealt with in A&E. You will become aware of them once you read my proposal for change.'

Erin rose from the chair, holding the folder against her chest like armour. 'I'll read it and get back to you,' she said.

'You do that,' he said with a half-smile that didn't meet his eyes.

She turned on her heel and was almost out the door when his deep baritone voice stopped her in her tracks.

'By the way, I checked the numbers in the parking area. Unless they are written in Braille, I am very much afraid a blind man could not see them.'

Erin turned back to face him. There was a hint of mockery in his sea-green gaze that made her scalp prickle in annoyance. 'I'll speak to the maintenance guy about having them repainted,' she said with the arch of an eyebrow. 'Or would you like him to paint arrows, or a big, fat, fluorescent "X" so you know exactly where to park?'

A tiny muscle moved next to his mouth. Erin wasn't sure if he was fighting anger or a smile; either way, it made him look even more attractive than he had last night. She felt the tiny flutter of her pulse, and a tingling of her flesh that made her breath catch as his eyes held hers.

'Just my number would be fine, thanks, Dr Taylor,' he said, and reached for his ringing mobile that was clipped on his belt. 'Excuse me. I have to get this.'

Erin spun away and closed the door with a sharp click behind her. She strode back to A&E; for the first time in her career she was immensely glad to see an overflowing waiting room.

It wasn't until Erin was back at her flat with her cat, Molly, on her lap that she picked up the document Eamon Chapman had given her that morning. She absently stroked Molly's thick fur as she read through the proposal, trying to ignore the sound of the sliding doors opening on the balcony next door. She had heard him come home about an hour after her. It gave her a slightly unsettled feeling to think of him on the other side of the wall. To her annoyance she found her thoughts drifting to what his routine might be: would he shower and change before dinner, or would he watch the news on television, perhaps have a beer or a glass of wine if he wasn't on call? Would he cook his own dinner or eat out? Did he have a partner? Was there a Mrs Chapman who would lie next to him in bed at night and be folded into his arms…?

Erin pulled away from her wayward thoughts and focused back on the words printed in front of her. So far there had been some sensible suggestions on streamlining triage and reducing the number of minor cases that should have been handled in general practice. The next section was on follow-through care. Her eyes narrowed as she read the plan for A&E doctors to conduct their own ward-rounds on the patients that had come into the hospital via the emergency department. As she read each word, she could feel a tide of panic rising inside her. She wasn't trained to sit by patients' bedsides and discuss the weather or their personal lives; she was trained to respond to emergencies, to stabilise patients before sending them on to definitive care. She would never be able to cope with all the names and faces, not to mention the added burden of thinking about patients and their lives outside of A&E. She put them out of her mind once they left the department. She had to, otherwise she would end up too involved, unable to remain at a clinical distance.

Erin tossed the document to one side and got to her feet, dislodging Molly, who gave an affronted miaow before turning her back to lick each of her paws with meticulous care.

The doors of the balcony beckoned and Erin slid them open to look out over the view of Sydney Harbour and the city on the opposite shore. Yachts were out, some with their colourful spinnakers up, looking like one-winged butterflies. Smaller craft bobbed about on the light swell and passenger ferries crisscrossed their way through the water, carrying people home from work or into the city for entertainment or dinner.

She gripped the balcony rail with an iron grip and lifted her face to the breeze, breathing in the salty air, wishing she could be on one of those yachts and sail away into the sunset.

'You wouldn't happen to have a cup of sugar, would you?' Eamon Chapman's voice sounded from her right.

Erin swivelled her head to look at him, her heart giving a little free fall. He was bare-chested, his legs encased in dark blue denim slung low on his lean hips. Every muscle on his chest and abdomen looked like it had been carved into place by a master craftsman. She had studied anatomy, yet not one of her textbooks would have done Dr Eamon Chapman justice. 'Um…sugar?'

His mouth tilted wryly. 'Yeah, that sweet stuff you put in coffee. I forgot to get some when I shopped on the way home.'

Erin brushed a strand of hair that the breeze had worked loose from her chignon away from her face. 'The shops are only a short walk away,' she pointed out.

'So you don't have any?' he asked, leaning on the dividing rail with his strong forearms. 'Sugar, I mean?'

Erin tried not to look at the way his biceps bulged as he leaned his weight on the railing. He was more or less at eye level, which was disconcerting to say the least. This close she could see tiny brown flecks in his green eyes that fanned out from his dark-as-ink pupils. 'I…I don't take sugar,' she said.

His mouth tilted even further. 'Sweet enough, huh?'

This time Erin was sure he was mocking her. 'I have five fillings,' she said primly. 'I am not keen on getting any more.'

'Didn't your mother teach you the importance of dental care?' he asked.

She schooled her features into a blank mask, hoping he hadn't noticed the slight flinch at the mention of her mother. 'It wasn't one of her strong points, no.'

Erin felt his silent scrutiny, as if he was reading her word by word, page by page. She wanted to go back inside but she felt inexplicably drawn to him, like tiny iron filings to a strong magnet.

'It's quite a coincidence, me moving in next door, don't you think?' he asked.

She gave a little shrug. 'There are three nurses and an orderly in this apartment block. Mosman's a convenient suburb. It's close to Sydney Met.'

'Are you renting or do you own your apartment?'

'The bank owns it,' she said. 'I work to keep up the payments.'

Erin had forgotten to close the balcony doors and Molly chose that moment to strut out like a model on a catwalk.

'I didn't realise you were allowed pets here,' he said, looking down as Molly began to weave around Erin's legs.

She grimaced as she scooped up the big fluffy bundle of fur. 'I–I've got special permission from the body corporate,' she lied.

Eamon Chapman cocked his head, as if debating whether to believe her. 'Isn't it cruel to house a cat indoors all the time?'

Erin stroked Molly's silky head. 'She's a Ragdoll. They prefer to be indoors.'

'What's its name?'

'Molly.'

'One of my sisters has a cat,' he said. 'Personally I'm a dog man, but yours looks cute.'

'Thank you.'

He straightened from the railing and stretched. Erin's eyes nearly popped out of her head, like popcorn from a hot pan, as each of his muscles rippled in response.

'Have you had time to look at my proposal?' he asked as his arms came back down to his sides.

Erin had to blink a couple of times to reorient herself. 'Um…yes, I have. I'm not sure it's going to work—that follow-through care thing—it's too complicated. A&E is too busy as it is to expect us to wander off to plump up patients' pillows on the wards.'

'You're missing the point, Dr Taylor,' he said. 'It's not about plumping up pillows; it's about treating the patient from start to finish as a person, not a statistic.'

'I don't treat patients as statistics.'

'Tell me the names of the last five patients you saw today.'

Erin stared at him as her mind went completely blank. She could barely remember faces, let alone names. It had been so frantic, especially when an elderly woman had been brought in with a cardiac arrest at the same time a head injury had arrived. Names hadn't been important; what had been important was saving lives that were hanging by a gossamer thread. 'I didn't have time to memorise their names,' she said, putting Molly down. 'My job is to save their lives.'

'Do you ever wonder what happens to them after they leave you?' he asked.

Erin didn't want to admit how much she wondered about them. She saw it as a weakness in herself, a frailty that should have been knocked out of her way back in medical school. She fought against her human feelings all the time; they kept her awake at night—the sea of faces that floated past like ghosts. 'Not really,' she said, her tone chilly. 'As I said, it's not my job.'

'You might want to have a rethink about that, Dr Taylor,' he said. 'The first trial ward-round begins tomorrow at the end of your shift.'

Erin forced her gaze to remain connected to his. 'Well, I can't see that working. You know as well as anyone that A&E shifts don't end according to the clock—they end when you finish treating your last patient, or at least get them to the point where you can hand them over to the next shift. You can't just breeze out to start chatting with folks on the ward.'

'You're so right. I am quite aware of that,' he said. 'If you read the plan properly, you would see that wind-up on your last patient starts an hour before your shift ends—that gives you at least part of the last hour to do ward follow-through.'

Erin gave him a mutinous look. 'Oh, so we just walk out an hour *before* our shift ends then, and I suppose the next shift starts an hour early to fill in the gap? Or maybe we just abandon A&E altogether for an hour. Look, you can hardly force already overworked staff to take on even more responsibility.'

'If you had read the proposal carefully, Dr Taylor, you would see that new arrangements do not mean more responsibility, just different responsibility. And, as far as implementing this plan, I'm not a great believer in using force to achieve anything,' he said. 'But I am the director, and I would like those working in my team to actually *be* a part of that team. The response from everyone else has been very positive, actually. I think you are going to find yourself out of touch with what everyone else is doing if you simply reject the department's policies.'

She arched her eyebrows. 'So, what do you plan to do, Dr Chapman? Hand-hold every A&E doctor until you're confident they're doing things your way?'

Eamon held her pert look, privately enjoying the way her burnt-toffee-brown eyes challenged his. Her defensive stance made him wonder why she was so against change. None of the other doctors he had briefed that morning had expressed any opposition to his proposal. In fact, three of them had cited cases where if such a plan had already been in place patient outcomes would have been better.

From what he had heard Erin Taylor was not one of the more social members of the department. Apparently she never joined in with regular drinks on Friday evenings at one of the local bars, and as far as he could tell she lived alone, apart from a contraband cat. She was prickly and unfriendly, yet her clinical management of patients was spot-on. She was competent and efficient, although one or two of the nurses had mentioned in passing her bedside manner needed work.

'I have certain goals I would like to achieve during my appointment,' he said. 'One of them is to improve overall outcomes for patients coming through A&E in this hospital. What you might not be aware of is how your expert work in A&E can be undone by isolating later management teams from the acute-care team. When was the last time you did a tertiary survey? It's mentioned in EMST and ATLS, but hardly ever happens. Sometimes injuries and clinical clues get missed in the wards. There is clear evidence that tertiary survey by the doctor who carried out the primary and secondary surveys is more likely to detect missed injuries, and so avoid complications which eat up beds and cost money.'

She continued to eyeball him in that 'I don't give a damn' way of hers. 'So, how long do you intend on propping up the public system before you scoot off for far more lucrative returns in the private sector?'

Eamon cocked an eyebrow at her. 'I could ask you the very same question.'

She held his look for a moment before turning to look at the harbour. The sun was low in the sky, casting a pinkish glow over the sails of the Opera House and the towering skyscrapers of the city on the opposite shore. 'I've thought about it plenty of times,' she said. 'But so far I haven't got round to doing anything about it.'

'You don't like change, do you, Dr Taylor?' Eamon asked.

She turned to look at him, her expression like curtains pulled across a window. 'I can deal with change when I think it's appropriate,' she said, and without another word slipped inside her apartment and shut the sliding doors—locking him out in more ways than one, he suspected.

CHAPTER TWO

ERIN had not long finished stitching a leg wound on a teenager the following morning when Tammy alerted her to a new admission.

'Forty-five-year-old male complaining of severe back pain,' Tammy said, reading from the notes she had taken down. 'His wife found him on the floor of the bathroom. He's nauseous and vomited prior to arriving in A&E.'

Erin twitched aside the curtains in bay four and introduced herself. 'Hello, I'm Dr Taylor. The triage nurse tells me you've got back pain. Can you describe it exactly?'

The man pointed to his left loin. 'Here...' he said somewhat breathlessly. 'Every couple of minutes... I....ahh...!' He writhed and groaned on the bed as his ashen-faced wife clutched one of his hands in hers.

'We'll give you something for the pain and nausea,' Erin said, administering morphine, buscopan and stemetil IV, with Tammy assisting.

'Is he going to be all right?' the man's wife asked.

'How long have you been unwell, Mr...' Erin glanced at the notes '...Aston?'

'I...I haven't been sick for years,' he said, and turned his head to his wife. 'Have I, love?'

Mrs Aston nodded. 'That's right, Doctor. He's never even taken a day off work in thirty-odd years. He's always been—'

'How's the pain now?' Erin asked as she clicked her pen open.

'Eased off a bit,' Mr Aston said, regaining some colour in his face as the pain-relief flooded his system.

'When did you first feel unwell?' Erin asked, pen poised over her patient-history clipboard.

'First thing this morning,' he said. 'I woke up to go to the toilet and then it hit me, didn't it, love?'

'I found him on the floor of the bathroom,' his wife put in. 'I nearly had a heart attack myself.'

Erin acknowledged the wife's statement with a movement of her lips that was neither a smile nor a grimace but something in between. 'I need you to give me a urine sample if you can manage it, Mr Aston,' she said, addressing the patient once more. 'I'd also like you to have an abdominal X-ray. The nurse will organise that while I see to another patient. Once we have the results of the urine sample, we'll know more.'

'Is it cancer?' Mrs Aston asked hollowly. 'Jeff used to smoke, didn't you, dear? He gave it up…what?…ten years ago now, it must be. I remember the day. It was when we went to—'

'We'll know more once we get the results back from the tests I've ordered,' Erin said briskly.

Tammy took over the care of the patient as Erin moved to the next bay. She parted the curtains to see Dr Chapman standing by the bedside of a young child with his mother. 'Oh, sorry,' Erin said. 'My patient must have been moved into another bay.'

Eamon gave her a formal smile which Erin suspected

was for the sake of the patient. 'Mrs Forster has been taken for a CT scan. This is Hamish, and his mother, Karen Young. Hamish here has had a persistent discharge from his right nostril for about a week, but this morning the discharge was blood-stained. We were about to have a look inside, weren't we, Hamish? You don't mind if Dr Taylor watches, do you? I bet she's never seen a braver young man around here.'

The young boy of about three stared wide-eyed but trustingly at Eamon, who picked up a nasal speculum and bright light. Erin was privately a little impressed at how biddable the child became under Eamon's care. She'd had a child with a foreign object up its nose only a month ago, and the floor above had heard its screams when she had tried to retrieve it. In the end she had handed the case over to the ear, nose and throat surgeon who had removed a plastic bead under general anaesthesia.

'There,' Eamon said as he showed the child and his mother the bright blue bead he had found. 'You were a champion, Hamish. I've seen kids twice your age who would have screamed the place down.'

'Weally?' Hamish asked, still a little bug-eyed.

'You betcha,' Eamon said, and then he turned and winked at the young mother. 'You can take him home now, Mrs Young. He's good to go. Just put the ointment Nurse will get for you up his nostril three times a day, and massage it in a bit, until you've finished the whole tube.'

Once the young mother and her son had left, Eamon turned to Erin. 'I'd like a word with you if you are free, Dr Taylor.'

Erin gave him a wary look. 'I have a patient who should be back from X-ray by now.'

'That would be Mr Aston next door?' he asked.

She flattened her mouth at his expression. 'I thought the plan was to have some sort of continuity of care around here,' she said, keeping her voice down in case the patient had returned. 'If I go off for a lengthy discussion with you, who's going to follow up Mr Aston?'

'Meet me in my office once you have finished assessing him,' he said, pushing the curtains aside. 'Unless, of course, anything urgent comes in.'

Erin blew out a breath once he moved past. It would be just her luck that today would be one of those quiet days, leaving her with no excuse to avoid another confrontation with him.

Mr Aston was being wheeled back to the examination bay when Erin returned, after responding to an HMO's phone call about another patient who had been admitted the day before.

Mr Aston's urine sample was positive for blood and his X-ray almost certainly showed a stone at the end of the right ureter. Erin ordered a rapid-sequence urinary-tract CT, which confirmed the finding, and she explained the results to the patient and his wife. 'You have renal colic, Mr Aston, which basically means you have a kidney stone. Very often stones pass spontaneously, but occasionally they don't.'

'What happens then?' Mrs Aston asked.

'If the stone doesn't pass, it may have to be removed under anaesthesia. We'd get a urologist to see you to do a cystoscopy—put a camera up the front passage into the bladder—and use a wire basket to grab the stone and pull it out.'

'Oh dear, it sounds horribly painful,' Mrs Aston said, grasping her husband's hand again.

'He'll be fine, Mrs Aston,' Erin said. 'The ENT specialist is one of the best in the city.'

Once she had left the patient's bay, Erin looked at the clock and thought longingly of a cup of tea and a sandwich, even one from the hospital cafeteria. But over an hour had passed since Eamon Chapman had asked her to meet him in his office, so rather than delay the inevitable any further she trudged through the department to where his office was located. She gave the door a quick knock, secretly wishing he had been called away, but she heard his deep voice commanding her to come in.

He was sitting behind his desk but rose to his feet as she came in. 'Have you had lunch?' he asked.

'No,' Erin said, wondering if he could read her mind or hear her stomach in this instance. 'But it can wait.'

'No need to. Why don't we head on down to the cafeteria and grab a sandwich now?' he asked.

She looked at him as if he had gone mad. 'I take it your plans to improve this hospital from top to bottom haven't quite made it to the cafeteria?' she said dryly.

He gave her a rueful smile. 'That bad, huh?'

She felt her lips twitch, but forced them back into line. 'Keep away from the salami and the chicken. We lost three staff members to a tandoori wrap three weeks ago.'

His dark brows lifted. '"Lost" as in…?'

'Lost as in sick for a week with a reportable disease,' she said. 'A couple of us had to do double shifts to cover them.'

His lips twitched this time, making his eyes crinkle up at the corners. 'There's a café on the other side of the car park,' he said. 'Does that have any black marks against it I should know about?'

'They do a mean salad sandwich with mung beans and alfalfa sprouts,' she said. 'And their coffee's passable.'

He picked up his mobile from the desk and clipped it to his belt. 'Let's give it a try. I'll just let Jan at reception know we'll be within paging distance.'

A few minutes later, sitting opposite Eamon Chapman in the café across from the hospital, Erin wondered how long it had been since she'd shared a meal with a man, even a colleague. She hadn't dated since medical school, and even then it had been an un-mitigated disaster. In the end she'd decided she wasn't cut out for the couples' scene. Most of the men she knew were complicated creatures with too much bag-gage—not that she could talk, given the veritable road-train she had brought with her from Adelaide. But this was hardly a date, she reminded herself. She was pretty certain Eamon Chapman had other things on his mind besides chatting her up. From what she could read from his expression, she was in for a dressing down if any-thing.

'So,' he said, leaning back in his chair to study her pensive features. 'How long have you been at Sydney Met?'

Erin was aware of his steady gaze on her as she toyed with the thick froth of her latte with a teaspoon. 'Five years,' she said, meeting his eyes for a brief moment. 'I spent a year in the States before that.'

'Travelling or working?'

'A bit of both,' she said.

'Did you grow up in Sydney?'

Erin's teaspoon gave a tiny clatter as she placed it back on the saucer. 'No. I grew up in South Australia. I moved to Sydney when I was a teenager.'

He took a sip of his cappuccino; her gaze was suddenly mesmerised by the tiny trace of chocolate that clung to his top lip before his tongue swept over his mouth to clear it. She swallowed a little restriction in her throat and quickly dropped her gaze, picking up her teaspoon again and stirring her latte with fierce concentration.

'So, do you have family here or back over there?' he asked.

Erin put her spoon back down and met his gaze. 'Look, I hate to be rude, but what's with the twenty questions?'

His eyes bored into hers for a tense second or two. 'I like to get a feel for the people I will be working with on a daily basis. It's an important part of being a leader, knowing the team's strengths and weaknesses.'

She screwed up her mouth in an embittered manner. 'Do you trust your own judgement on that, or are you usually swayed by others' opinions?'

He accepted her comment with an unreadable look. 'I lean towards the "innocent until proven guilty" philosophy where possible.'

She gave a little snort and reached for her coffee again. 'Yeah, well, I bet it didn't take long for some members of the jury to swing your opinion.'

'What makes you say that?' he asked.

Erin gave her shoulders a gentle shrug. 'Gut feeling; instinct; experience.'

'I wanted to have a word with you about how you handled Mr Aston,' he said after a short silence.

Erin's gaze flicked back to his. 'It was straight-out renal colic. He's got a stone the size of a marble. He's not going to pass it without surgical intervention.'

'I'm not for a moment questioning your diagnosis,

Dr Taylor,' Eamon said. 'But I think you could improve on your handling of accompanying relatives. Coming into A&E is stressful for both patients *and* relatives.'

She set her mouth into a defensive line. 'My job is to treat the patient, not pander to their entourage.'

Eamon put his coffee cup back in its saucer, his eyes holding hers. 'Listen, managing the relatives is *part* of treating the patient. Stressed relatives worsen patients' stresses. And accompanying relatives are usually going to be the patient's carers afterwards. One, they need to be well informed. Two, if they are stressed out and decompensate, they won't be good carers. That means more time for patients in hospital, more hospital expense and more loss to the community. I've only been in the department less than twenty-four hours and I have already heard several complaints about your handling of relatives, yesterday's threat of litigation being a case in point.'

Her slim jaw tightened. 'Mrs Haddad's suit will be rejected as soon as the medical council read through my notes and realise the extent of her son's injuries.'

'That is most certainly the case; however, the whole thing may well have been avoided if you had softened your approach.'

'You know nothing of my approach,' she said, shooting him a livid glare. 'You weren't there trying to save the boy's life. When someone is bleeding out before your eyes, it's not exactly the time to ask how his mother or his family are feeling, for God's sake.'

Eamon leaned forward in his chair, his arms resting on the table. Erin moved back, folding her arms across her chest, her chin at a defiant height. 'As you are now aware, I was in the bay next to you when you were assessing Mr Aston,' he said. 'His wife was clearly distressed to see her normally healthy husband in such a state. A reassuring word to her wouldn't have gone astray, not cutting her off in mid-sentence.'

Erin rolled her eyes, and, pushing back her chair, got to her feet in one angry movement. 'I haven't got time for this. I've got patients to see.'

His green eyes hit hers. 'Sit down, Dr Taylor.'

Erin's hands gripped the chair-back with white-knuckled fingers. She was so tempted to shove the chair back underneath the table to drive home her point, but the steely look in his eyes forestalled her.

Several tense seconds passed before she reluctantly gave in. She sat back down, crossing her arms and legs as she sent him a querulous look. 'You said you'd had other complaints about me,' she said. 'Am I allowed to know who they were from?'

He leaned back in his chair, but the hardened look hadn't softened in his eyes. 'That would be unprofessional of me. The complaints were made in confidence; in fact, they weren't even official, just passing comments. No one is out to get you, Dr Taylor, far from it. Generally the staff speak very highly of you, on a professional level.'

'So my bedside manner needs some work,' she said with a petulant huff of her shoulder. 'Pardon me for putting patients' lives in front of politeness.'

'I don't see why you can't manage both,' he said. 'Or do you have a particular reason for being so prickly with everyone?'

Erin felt the probe of his gaze and had to work hard to maintain eye contact. Something about him made her feel exposed. Even though she had only met him the day before, that intelligent, penetrating gaze of his had a habit of catching her off guard. He was seeing things she didn't want him to see, things she had fought hard to keep hidden. She liked her life in its neat little compartments, but she felt as if he was threatening her stronghold, insisting on her being someone she was not, nor ever could be. 'I'm not interested in winning the latest popularity contest,' she said. 'If people don't like me, I don't let it worry me. I have better things to do with my time.'

'Do you live alone, apart from your cat?' he asked.

Erin frowned. 'I thought we were here to discuss issues to do with work, not my private life.'

Eamon draped one arm over the back of the chair that was next to his; his gaze continued to hold hers. 'Sometimes one's private life can have an impact on their professional one.'

She gave him an arch look. 'Sometimes one's boss can put his nose where it is not welcome.'

Eamon felt his lips flicker with a smile. 'I'm not just your boss, Dr Taylor, I am also your neighbour. That blurs the boundaries a bit, don't you think?'

'Not for me,' she said with a flinty glare.

He leaned forward again, his eyes still locked on hers. 'As I said earlier, I don't like the heavy-handed approach, but if it's called for I am not afraid to use it. If you don't lift your game, I will have to take appropriate action.'

She eyeballed him back. 'If you want to fire me, go right ahead, but if you do I'll have the unfair-dismissal commission on your back before you can say Code Blue.'

Eamon felt a rush of blood to his groin at her feisty words. She was like a spitting cat, all claws and hiss, making him want to tame that wild streak by pressing his own mouth to her snarling one. He wondered if anyone had been game enough to come within touching distance of her. She sent out keep-away-from-me vibes like soundwaves. For some reason he found that incredibly attractive. His three younger sisters would think he was crazy taking on someone like Erin Taylor; they were hanging out for a sweet sister-in-law they could take shopping and do girly things with. Somehow he couldn't see the pint-sized Dr Taylor with her touch-me-not glare and barbed tongue going down too well with his touchy-feely family.

'Eamon?' A high female voice sounded from behind their table.

Erin turned her head to see one of the nurses from the surgical ward approaching, bringing with her a wave of heady perfume that irritated Erin's nostrils.

'Hi, Sherrie,' Eamon, said, rising to his feet and sweeping the woman into a brief, hard hug. He held her from him to look down at her flushed features. 'How're you doing? I've been meaning to call you, but things have been pretty crazy since I got back from London.'

'Don't worry about it,' the woman called Sherrie said, with a beaming smile. 'Gosh, you look fabulous. Jet lag and hard work must suit you.'

Eamon gave a self-deprecating smile before turning to introduce Erin. 'Sherrie, do you know Dr Erin Taylor from A&E?'

Sherrie held out her hand. 'No, I don't think we've met properly. I've seen you around, though. Nice to meet you.'

Erin briefly placed her hand in the other woman's before pulling away. 'Thank you,' she said. 'You too.'

'So…' Sherrie turned back to Eamon. 'When are you free for a meal or a drink or something? Where are you staying? Have you bought a house or an apartment?'

Eamon grinned at the barrage of questions, holding up his hands as if to ward them off. 'One at a time, Sherrie. Yes, a meal would be great, and I'm renting my mate Tim Yeoman's apartment in Mosman until the renovations are completed on my house at Balmoral Beach. Tim's still on sabbatical in Edinburgh.'

Sherrie took a pen out of her uniform pocket and scribbled her number and address on a napkin from the table. She handed it to him and smiled. 'Here are my details,' she said. 'I've changed my number since I last saw you. Call me any time. It will be great to hear all about your time in the UK.'

Eamon folded the napkin and put it in the breast pocket of his shirt. 'Thanks, Sherrie; I'll see what I can do for next week. I'm still unpacking, otherwise I'd organise something sooner.'

'No problem,' Sherrie said, and glanced at her watch. 'Oops. Gotta dash. I'm meant to be in Surg A by now. Congratulations on the new job, Eamon. You're exactly what this place needs to whip it into shape.' She turned and smiled at Erin. 'See you around, Erica.'

'Erin,' Erin corrected her.

'Oh, sorry, I'm hopeless with names.' And then, with another beaming smile aimed at Eamon, Sherrie left.

Erin pushed her half-drunk latte away. 'A love interest of yours?' she asked.

He sat back down and drained the contents of his cup before he answered. 'We dated a couple of times a few years ago. Nothing too serious, and fortunately we managed to remain friends after we called it quits.'

'It looks to me like she would like a re-run,' Erin said, not quite able to stop herself from sounding slightly churlish.

One of his dark brows lifted. 'Is that feminine intuition or something else?'

She was the first to shift her gaze. 'What else could it be?' she asked. 'You're not exactly my type.'

'Oh really?' he said. 'What is your type?'

Erin wished she hadn't started the conversation. She could feel her colour rising as the silence stretched and stretched. How could she answer such a question? She didn't have a type. She didn't even have a social life. She had a cat and a career and a cartload of reasons to keep her life as simple as possible. 'I have to get going,' she said, making a show of looking at her watch. 'I don't want another long day.'

'Big plans for this evening?' he asked as he rose to his feet.

Erin wondered if he was making fun of her. To an attractive man with women falling over themselves to book him for a date, her life must seem pretty dull in comparison. 'Yes, as a matter of fact,' she lied. 'I'm meeting someone after work.'

'About what we discussed over coffee…' Eamon began as he accompanied her back to the hospital.

'Don't worry, Dr Chapman,' she said before he could continue. 'I'll get working on winning friends and influencing people right now.'

Eamon watched as she stalked off down the corridor, her head down, her shoulders hunched and her face like a brewing storm. 'You do that, Dr Taylor,' he murmured, and, blowing out a breath, made his way back to his office.

'Aren't you supposed to be doing the trial ward-round with Dr Chapman?' Lydia Hislop, one of the nurses who regularly worked with Erin, asked. 'The others left over half an hour ago.'

Erin frowned as she checked through the patient's notes she was reading, barely registering what the nurse had said. 'When did Mrs Fuller have a second shot of pethidine?' She glanced at the nurse. 'I don't remember signing for it.'

Lydia peered at the notes, her forehead creasing over a frown. 'That's your signature, isn't it?'

Erin felt a cold hand of unease press against the base of her spine. She closed the patient folder and let out a long, unsteady breath. 'I must be working way too hard,' she muttered. 'I can't even remember what day it is.'

'Tell me about it,' Lydia said with an empathetic eye-roll. 'Have you got time to see Mr Boyle in bay five, or should I get one of the night-duty staff to deal with it?'

Erin glanced at her watch. The ward-round, even if she had wanted to attend, would be winding up by now; it would be over altogether by the time she made it up to the appropriate floor. 'I'll see him,' she said. 'That's the one with the suspected appendix, right?'

'Yes, I've got his history here,' Lydia said, handing her a file. 'He's been in before for a resection of gangrenous bowel about two years ago.'

'That should make for interesting surgery,' Erin said. 'Who's the surgeon on call?'

'Mr Gourlay,' Lydia said. 'Your all-time favourite.'

This time is was Erin who rolled her eyes. 'Maybe I should have gone on that ward-round after all.'

When Erin got home from work, Molly wound her plump body around her legs, mewing in delight. Erin smiled and scooped her up, burying her face in the cat's luxurious fur. The phone rang inside her bag, and she gently put Molly down to answer it. When she saw the number on the screen, she felt a hand of dread clutch at her insides. 'Hello, Mum,' she said in a flat tone.

'Ezzie, I need your help,' Leah Taylor said. 'Things have been tough just lately, you know how it is.'

Erin whooshed out an impatient sigh. 'No, Mum, strange as it may seem, I don't know how it is.'

'There's no need to be nasty,' Leah said. 'All I want is a bit of cash to get me through until my next pension payment.'

Erin began pacing; it was almost unconscious every time she spoke with her mother. Back and forth she went across the carpet, like a caged animal desperate for freedom. She could even see the slightly worn area when she'd last vacuumed. 'Mum, you know what the social worker said about me giving you money all the time,' she said. 'You just shoot it up or drink it.'

'I'm going straight now, Ez,' her mother said. 'I haven't touched a drop for three days.'

Erin rolled her eyes. 'And what about Bob or Bill or Brad, or whatever his name is? Is he going straight too?'

'Just because you can't pull a man doesn't give you the right to slag me off. If you would just tart yourself up a bit you wouldn't be living all alone with just a stupid cat for company.'

Erin felt anger rising in her like the froth of a soda poured too rapidly, threatening to overflow the glass of her control. She had to fight her temper back, knowing from experience it never worked with her mother. There was no hope of a rational conversation with someone in the grip of addiction. She had learned that earlier than any child should have to learn. Some people loved their fix more than their children. Leah Taylor was one of them. The drink and the drugs would always come first, her unsavoury boyfriends a close second. 'Mum, I'm going to hang up now, OK?' she said in a cool, calm voice. 'I'll call you in a couple of days.'

'How can you turn your back on your own mother?' Leah asked in a whining tone.

Erin closed her eyes as she thought of all the times her mother had abandoned her, leaving her to fend for herself until the authorities had finally stepped in. Years of being shunted from one foster home to another, with short periods of being reunited with her mother in some of Leah's all-too-brief periods of sobriety. Yes, Erin could easily turn her back on her mother. It was either that or get hurt all over again. 'I'll call you later, Mum,' she said again.

'Selfish little cow,' Leah snapped. 'You're just like your father.'

'And that would be…?' Erin asked pointedly.

Her mother slammed the phone down.

CHAPTER THREE

ERIN wasn't sure why she went to that particular movie at that particular cinema, but at the time she had figured it was much better than spending the evening alone with her demons. The film was an art-house foreign-language one she had read a review about in one of the weekend papers. She took her seat and sipped at a diet soda; she barely read the subtitles, she just looked at the images flashing across the screen while her thoughts drifted elsewhere.

When she came out of the cinema the streets were crowded with people on their way home from dinner, or on their way to nightclubs for drinking and dancing. The noisy chatter and laughter of everyone having a good time as they enjoyed the balmy autumn evening made Erin wish she hadn't come out after all.

She had never felt more alone in her life.

Eamon picked up his takeaway meal from his favourite restaurant, thrilled that the same people were still running it since he had left to work in the UK a couple of years ago. Right now he could think of nothing better than a cold beer and a madras curry, maybe watching some cricket on television or catching up on some current affairs on the Net.

He suddenly noticed a slight figure in the small crowd that was milling out of the local cinema, her shiny chestnut hair loose about her face instead of tightly pulled back. She was wearing jeans and a loose shirt over a camisole top, with ballet flats on her feet. Her eyes were downcast as she weaved her way through the knots of people, as if she didn't want to be noticed.

Eamon was on his way to her when he saw a boisterous couple coming the other way jostle against her, almost knocking her over.

'Hey, watch where you're going,' the young male half of the couple said belligerently.

Eamon quickly broke through the crowd and put his arm around Erin's waist, pulling her close to his side. 'Sorry I'm late, sweetheart,' he said. Then, turning to look at the obstreperous pair, he gave them the full force of his commanding gaze. 'Is there a problem here?'

The couple exchanged a glance, the young man eventually giving a shrug. 'It's cool, mate. I guess I wasn't watching where I was going.'

'That's what I thought,' Eamon said, and stood with his arm still around Erin's waist until they had moved on.

Erin felt the nerves beneath her skin tingle with feelings she had never felt before. The weight of his arm was unfamiliar, but not in any way unpleasant. With him standing so close to her she could smell his light citrus-based aftershave; she could even see the individual points of stubble on his jaw. The most primal feelings swept over her. No one had ever sprung to protect her before. It awakened such deep yearnings she had trouble disguising how affected she was. To cover her vulnerability, she stepped out of his embrace and dusted herself off, as if his touch had contaminated her in some way. 'Thanks,' she mumbled. 'But the sweetheart thing was a bit over-the-top, don't you think?'

His mouth curved upwards in a smile. 'I don't know,' he said. 'It worked, didn't it?'

Erin found her lips wanting to return his smile, but she controlled them by biting the inside of her mouth.

'So, where's your date?' he asked, looking up and down the street before returning his gaze to hers.

'What date? Oh...' She felt her face colour again. 'Um...they couldn't make it at the last minute.'

'Another doctor, huh?'

'Um...' She looked away. 'No. Just a... Someone who couldn't make it.'

'Story of my life,' he said with a hint of wryness.

Erin looked at him. '*You* got stood up?' Her voice came out slightly incredulous.

'You didn't turn up for the first ward-round,' he said, skewering her with his gaze.

Erin bit her lip and turned away. 'I know. I'm sorry, I had a tough case to deal with. I lost track of time.'

'I realise it won't always be possible to attend each one, but the plan overall is to improve continuity of care,' he said. 'Today's round showed up a few holes in the system, so it will be good to work on those. I can fill you in on what went on so you don't feel out of the loop.'

Erin had always felt out of the loop, but she didn't tell him so. She hadn't gone to the right school, and she certainly hadn't come from the right family. She didn't mix with the high-flyers; she just got on with her job, hoping to make a difference where she could. 'You seem pretty sure this set-up will work,' she said. 'Is this new system something you experienced overseas?'

'Yes and no,' he said. 'I've worked in several A&E

departments now, and I've seen a lot of avoidable problems occur because communication with the medical staff in A&E stopped the moment the patient was rolled out the door of the department—problems that would have been avoided with a structured follow-through plan involving the staff who did the primary assessment.'

Erin suddenly noticed the takeaway bag he was carrying. 'I'm sorry, I didn't realise I was holding you up from your dinner.'

'You're not holding me up,' he said. 'I was just on my way home. Did you drive or walk?'

'I walked,' she said. 'Parking is always a pain down here at this time of night.'

'Like most cities,' he agreed. 'I'll walk back with you. Have you had dinner? I've got enough to share if you'd like to join me.'

Erin felt her cheeks flush. 'Oh no…I wouldn't want to intrude.'

'You're not intruding. Besides, I can tell you how the ward-round went while we eat.'

Erin wanted to refuse but the thought of the rest of the evening alone was suddenly not as welcome as it had been earlier. She told herself she should at least be polite to Eamon after he had come to her rescue so gallantly. Surely she owed him an hour or two of her time? 'Thanks, that would be nice,' she said, glancing at him shyly.

Following the short walk back, Eamon activated the security pass to the apartment block and waited for her to precede him. The elevator ride was swift but to Erin it felt as if it was taking for ever. She didn't know what to say; she didn't even know where to stand. She shifted her weight from foot to foot, half-leaning, half-standing against the bare wall of the elevator. She felt awkward,

gauche and out of place, certain he was wondering what
was wrong with her. He was probably used to the most
sophisticated of women, wining and dining them in
world-class restaurants. No doubt he bedded them as
well, taking pleasure where he found it, almost certainly giving it back one-hundredfold. She kept her arms
folded across her chest but even so she could still feel
where his arm had been about her waist.

She began to imagine what it would feel like to have
his touch on other parts of her body—her mouth, for
instance. His mouth was a sensual one, the lower lip
fuller than the top one, making her lips start to tingle in
anticipation of feeling its firmness against hers. Would
he kiss softly or firmly? Would he cup her face or hold
her by the shoulders? Would he...?

The doors of the elevator opening catapulted her out
of her wayward thoughts. With her colour still high, she
moved past Eamon as he held the doors open with the
strong band of his arm, her heart doing little skips in her
chest as she breathed in his scent once more. She felt
ashamed of her reaction, and hoped to God he wasn't
picking up on it. How foolish of her to be so taken in by
good looks and easy charm. He was her boss, for goodness' sake! What sort of a fool would she be to compromise her professionalism by becoming involved with
a colleague? In any case, given her background, how
soon would he stay interested in her? She could hardly
take him home to meet her mother and her latest junkie
boyfriend. Men like Eamon Chapman dated women
from the right side of the tracks, not trailer-park misfits.

'I'm sorry the place is still a bit of a mess,' Eamon
said as he opened his apartment door. 'I should be an
expert at unpacking by now; I've done it enough times.'

Not as many times as me, Erin thought as she followed him inside. 'Can I do anything to help?' she asked.

'No, just take a seat and I'll get some plates,' he said. 'Would you like a glass of wine? I've got red and white, or beer if you'd prefer.'

'I'm not much of a drinker, so don't open anything specially.'

'One glass of wine won't hurt you,' he said, taking a bottle of chilled white wine from the fridge. 'It'll help you relax.'

Erin pulled at her bottom lip with her teeth. 'Is it that obvious?'

He gave her a reassuring smile. 'Hey, don't be so hard on yourself. That drunken jerk would have frightened most people. He was probably pretty harmless, but these days you never can tell.'

Erin hadn't given the inebriated young man another thought. It was the stone-cold sober, gorgeous one standing in front of her right now that was her real concern. 'I guess I should think about taking some self-defence classes,' she said, taking the glass of wine he handed her.

'Not a bad idea,' he said. 'You're so tiny it wouldn't take much to knock you off your feet.'

Erin felt a shivery feeling move down her spine. How could one casual, throwaway comment make her feel so utterly feminine? She buried her nose in her glass, keeping her gaze averted from his while her heart did funny little somersaults behind her ribcage.

Eamon found plates and cutlery and soon had the food dished up and placed on the kitchen table. 'There you go,' he said, handing her a napkin.

'Thank you,' she said. 'This is very good of you. I was going to have cheese on toast.'

'It's a good standby, I'll grant you,' he said. 'But it'll hardly give you the energy for the sort of hours we work.'

'No, I guess not.'

Eamon watched as she picked delicately at the food. She seemed ill at ease but he couldn't quite decide if it was his company or the experience on the street earlier. He couldn't help comparing her to his three boisterous, extroverted sisters who each sailed through life making numerous friends as they went. Erin Taylor had a guarded air about her, as if she didn't warm to people easily, nor expect them to warm to her. 'So, what did you think of the film?' he asked.

She glanced up from her plate, blinking at him for a moment. 'Film?'

He offered her more curry but she shook her head. He served himself some more as he said, 'The French film you went to see. I saw you amongst the crowd coming out of the cinema. What was it like?'

'Oh…' She put down her fork and dabbed at her mouth with her napkin, not quite meeting his eyes. 'It was…OK.'

'Worth seeing?'

She put her napkin down and briefly met his eyes. 'The cinematography was wonderful.'

'And the storyline?'

She gnawed at her lip in an engaging, little-girl-lost manner. 'Um…it was…it was…'

Eamon laughed. 'It's all right; I get the picture—literally.'

'Oh no,' she said, looking a little shocked. 'I didn't mean to imply it was not worth seeing. It's just that I had other things on my mind…' She gave a little sigh that seemed to come from deep inside her. 'Look, I'm really sorry I didn't make it to the ward-round. I know you probably think I deliberately missed it but something came up and I thought I should attend to it.'

'It's cool, Erin,' he said, watching as she blushed when he spoke her name for the first time.

Her gaze fell away from his. 'I…I guess I should get going,' she said, pushing back her chair. 'Thanks for the meal, it was lovely.'

'You don't have to rush off, surely?' he said, suddenly realising how much he wanted her to stay. 'I'll put the kettle on for coffee.'

She appeared to hesitate, making him wonder if she was as reluctant to leave as he was for her to go. The thought secretly thrilled him. They were two single adults with time on their hands. Sure, they worked together, but that didn't mean they couldn't keep their professional lives separate from their private ones. He'd had relationships with colleagues before; it took a little juggling at times, but he was at a time in his life when he was looking for more. He wasn't entirely sure Erin Taylor was the one to give him the whole package, but she had certainly spiked his interest with her shy, almost gauche manner. She intrigued him, and not a lot of women did that any more. He saw through the flirty come-and-get-me wiles too easily, having witnessed his sisters bring too many men to their knees. No, Erin Taylor was something else—something he was starting to realise was worth investigating a little further.

'One coffee, then,' she said, getting up to help clear the dishes.

Eamon took the plates from her, and their hands met briefly. He saw the way her pupils flared, as if he had sent a current straight from his body to hers. He felt the same current fire through him, lighting a fire in his groin that flickered and then roared. His eyes went to her mouth, the soft cushion of it tempting him to lean forward to taste it. She had not once in the whole time he had known her smiled at him. Suddenly it seemed imperative that she did. 'Has anyone told you what lovely brown eyes you have?' he asked.

She suddenly stepped back. 'I've changed my mind about that coffee,' she said tightly. 'I need to feed Molly.'

Eamon bit back a curse as she stalked to the door. He had never been rejected for a cat before and it stung—badly. 'Erin...' He raked his hand through his hair, feeling as if he had time-travelled back to his hormone-raging teens. 'I didn't mean to offend you. I was just—'

She turned at the door, fixing him with a cold, hard stare. 'You didn't,' she said. 'I just have other priorities right now.' And with that she left.

'Are you sure you want to work a full week of nights?' the nursing supervisor in charge of the rosters asked Erin the next morning. 'I thought you hated night duty.'

'I do, but then who doesn't?' Erin said. 'I just thought I'd get them all over with at once for a change.'

'This doesn't have anything to do with the new director, does it?' Gwen asked, narrowing her gaze playfully. 'I heard he's turning everything upside down in the department.'

Erin felt her cheeks heating. 'I am sure he's well intentioned,' she said, keeping her voice flat with disinterest.

'He's rather gorgeous looking,' Gwen said. 'If I was twenty years younger, I would be making sure I was doing mirror shifts with him.'

Erin took her duty roster from the printer, keeping her expression blank. 'I'd better get going. The waiting room was empty when I left, but who knows how long that will last?'

It lasted all of ten minutes. By the time Erin got back there was a line-up at the door and she didn't surface from assessing, treating and admitting until it was mid-afternoon.

She was on her way to the doctors' room on the third floor when she ran into one of the senior surgeons, Arthur Gourlay. She mentally rolled her eyes and forced her face into a polite mask. 'Good afternoon, Mr Gourlay,' she said.

'What's the meaning of sending me patients without adequate pain-relief?' he blustered without preamble. 'I've had the family on my back for the last hour.'

Erin frowned. 'Which patient are you referring to?'

'That woman you admitted late this morning,' he said. 'The elderly one with bowel obstruction, Mrs Pappas.'

Erin clearly remembered ordering pethidine for the woman in question; she had signed for it, as per hospital regulations, although in this case the nurse on duty had administered it as Erin had been called to another emergency. 'Mr Gourlay, Mrs Pappas had pethidine in A&E and soon after was sent up to Surg B. If she was still in pain, I was unaware of it, as she ceased to be my responsibility once she was admitted to the ward.'

'This is not the first time this has happened,' Arthur Gourlay said. 'I'm going to have a word to the director about it. He's got a point about this follow-through thing. It seems once a patient is out of A&E they cease to exist.'

Erin felt her back stiffen. 'That's not true. It's just that A&E was full all morning. Mrs Pappas was properly assessed and given pain-relief as per my instructions. You can check my notes if you don't believe me.'

'What seems to be the problem?' Eamon Chapman asked from behind her.

Erin felt the hairs on the back of her neck rise as she turned to face him and her heart gave a funny little skip when his eyes met hers.

'Dr Taylor has developed a habit of sending patients to the ward without adequate pain-relief,' Arthur Gourlay said. 'She seems to think—'

'That is not true,' Erin jumped in defensively.

'Arthur, I will handle this,' Eamon said calmly. 'I need to speak to Dr Taylor about another matter in any case.'

Arthur gave Erin a pompous sneer. 'It's about time someone pulled you into line.' He strode off down the corridor, muttering under his breath as he went.

Eamon swung his gaze to Erin. 'What was all that about?' he asked.

Her cheeks were glowing with anger and her body was stiff, as if she was fighting to keep it contained. 'Arthur Gourlay accused me of not administering pain-relief to a patient this morning,' she said. 'But I clearly remember writing it up.'

'What sort of delay was there before the patient was transferred to the ward?' he asked, stepping aside to allow an orderly go past with an empty gurney.

'I don't know,' she said. 'I was called to another emergency; a cardiac arrest came in and I was with him for the next hour.'

Another orderly was coming down the corridor, this

time with a patient in a wheelchair. 'Let's go to the doctors' room and discuss this out of the hearing of the public,' Eamon said.

He shouldered open the door a metre or so down the corridor, waiting until she went in first. The room was thankfully empty except for the fragrant aroma of coffee brewing on a machine next to the sink.

'Coffee?' he asked.

She hesitated, as if she didn't want to prolong the meeting any longer than she had to, but he saw the way her eyes glanced at the coffee machine and the little up-and-down movement of her slim throat in anticipation of that first reviving swallow.

'I'm going to have one, so I might as well pour you one as well,' he said. 'How do you have it?'

'Black.'

'No sugar?'

She gave him a pointed look. 'Five fillings, remember?'

He smiled lopsidedly. 'Right, how could I forget?' He handed her a mug of the brew and added, 'Is that why you never smile?'

She took the mug with fingers that fumbled in the handover, her eyes averted from his. 'I smile when I think it's appropriate,' she said. 'A&E doesn't seem the place to be grinning like an idiot.'

'So what's the deal with Arthur Gourlay?' Eamon asked after a little pause. 'He's seems to have some pretty heavy angst towards you.'

She gave him a direct look. 'Arthur is like a lot of men with oversized egos. He doesn't like it when he doesn't get his own way.'

Eamon cocked an eyebrow. 'Let me guess, he asked you out and you turned him down?'

Her eyes widened in surprise. 'How did you know? Did he say something to you?'

He shook his head. 'No, but I recognise the signs of a man scorned.'

She looked down at the contents of her mug. 'About last night…'

'Forget about it. I have.'

She looked up at him, her brown eyes wary. 'I wouldn't want you to get the wrong idea.'

'Dr Taylor,' he said. 'We met by chance, we shared a casual meal. That's all it was: a neighbourly get-together.'

She pressed her lips together. 'Right. Of course.' She put her coffee down. 'I'd better get back.'

'Before you go,' Eamon said. 'The pain-management issue Arthur spoke about—he mentioned this has happened before.'

Her eyes took on that guarded look again. 'Are you accusing me of something, Dr Chapman?'

'What would I be accusing you of?' he asked.

She held his look, her mouth pulled tight. 'I have followed the drug protocol scrupulously.'

'No one has suggested you haven't.'

Erin wondered if she should mention the incident the day before where she couldn't recall signing the second shot of pethidine for a patient. But surely that would make her look incompetent if she told him she couldn't remember what she had done and when? 'I suppose you're going to say this proves how important your follow-through plan is,' she said.

'It's pretty obvious there are some gaps in the system,' he said. 'But that's why I'm here to sort them out. I noticed you didn't make it to the second breakfast meeting. We'll be holding them all week and next until I have each A&E staff member up to date.'

'I've read through the document you gave me,' Erin said. 'And, depending on what happens this afternoon, I'll try and make the ward-round.'

'I would appreciate it, Dr Taylor,' he said. 'By the way, I thought you might like to know, Mrs Haddad— the mother of the young man who died of the stab-wound—has withdrawn her complaint.'

Erin felt her shoulders go down in relief. 'I'm very sorry for her loss, but I tried everything I could to save him. It was just too late.'

'I think she came to realise that,' he said. 'It's sad, isn't it? The waste of a young life—all that potential gone to waste.'

Erin kept her expression blank. 'There's enough drug education around to warn people of the dangers.'

He studied her for a moment with that piercing green gaze. 'You don't have empathy for someone with a drug problem?' he asked.

'Look, Dr Chapman,' she said, expelling a breath of impatience. 'There are lots of really ill patients who need our care. People who self-abuse clog up the system and take valuable resources away from others who are unwell through no fault of their own.'

'It's not our place to make value judgements on patients who come in for treatment,' he said. 'There are a host of reasons why people get hooked on drugs or alcohol. They deserve the same level of care and priority afforded any other patient.'

'I'm not for a moment saying I would treat anyone differently,' she said. 'I just wish more people would take responsibility for their own health.'

'I understand the frustration; I feel it myself at times,' Eamon said. 'But there is only a limited amount of funds to go around. We have to do what we can with what we have.'

There was a beat or two of silence.

Erin heard the ticking of the clock on the wall and the white-noise hum of the refrigerator as it reset its thermostat. She also felt sure she could hear the beating of her heart. It was booming in her chest like a kettle drum with a beat that was as unsteady as it was rapid. She sent the tip of her tongue out to moisten her dry lips, her stomach giving an unexpected little kick of excitement when she saw his gaze slowly descend to her mouth.

Time froze for a moment, and then began to swell with promise...

The door behind Erin suddenly opened and a female voice chimed, 'Oops, sorry, I didn't meant to disturb you both.'

Erin turned and faced the female registrar. 'You weren't disturbing anything,' she mumbled, and quickly made her way out the door, her face feeling as if it was on fire.

CHAPTER FOUR

ERIN was in her kitchen feeding Molly that evening when she heard the sliding doors of next door's balcony open. Her skin automatically tightened, and her heart gave a little thump as she heard the click-clack of foot-steps on the tiles.

'Gosh, Eamon,' a feminine voice said. 'It's an abso-lutely awesome view from here. I wish you'd let me move in with you. Won't you reconsider? *Please?*'

Erin pressed her spine flat against the pantry door as she shamelessly eavesdropped.

'No way, Stephanie,' Eamon said, although his tone was full of warmth. 'We'd be at each other's throats within days.'

'You're so heartless,' the young woman said. 'I don't know why I still love you.'

'It's your job, that's why,' he said.

Erin silently fumed. What an arrogant playboy! No doubt he had woman after woman hanging around for his attention. How annoying, if she was going to have to listen to him every night wooing his latest conquest. She had thought the dope-smoking university students were bad, but living next door to a modern-day Lothario was going to be completely sickening. What if she had to listen to him…? *Oh no, don't even think about it,* she reproached herself sternly. She would get some heavy-duty earplugs and turn up the music or something.

All went quiet for a moment and Erin edged away from the pantry door and sneaked a peek. Her eyes rounded in shock and disgust. The girl called Stephanie was barely out of her teens. What a jerk!

'Have you met any of your neighbours?' Stephanie asked, brushing back her mane of glossy dark hair and looking up at Eamon coquettishly.

Erin stiffened.

'Yes, I have, actually.'

'And?' Stephanie planted one hand on her hip and tilted her head at him.

'And it's none of your business,' he said. 'Anyway, she might be listening.'

Erin sucked in a breath and quickly flattened herself back against the pantry door.

'She?' Stephanie's voice rose. 'There's a woman living next-door? How old? What does she look like? Is she single? Is she nice?'

Eamon laughed. '"She" is one of the doctors at Sydney Met.'

Completely heartless, Erin thought. Had he no consideration for poor Stephanie's feelings? What if the poor girl was in love with him? After all, she had practically begged him to allow her to move in with him.

'Come on, Eamon,' Stephanie pleaded. 'Tell me the rest. You could be dating her for all I would know.'

As if! Erin thought.

'One shared curry hardly constitutes a date,' Eamon said.

'So you've had dinner with her?'

Erin couldn't quite make out the tone of Stephanie's voice. She didn't sound disappointed—incredulous, perhaps, but certainly not heartbroken.

'Just the once but it didn't go so well,' Eamon said. 'Anyway, she's not my type. She's uptight and prickly. And she's stubborn.'

Stephanie laughed. 'Ho, ho, ho, Mr Kettle, have you checked out your shade of black lately?'

'Cute,' Eamon said in a droll tone. 'Real cute.'

'Seriously, though, Eamon,' Stephanie went on. 'Is she pretty?'

Erin held her breath.

'So-so,' Eamon said. 'If you go for that girl-next-door look.'

So-so? Erin fumed. *So-so?*

Stephanie chuckled again. 'So, when do you think I can meet her to check her out for myself?' she asked.

'Well, if you stand over here where I'm standing, you can get quite a clear view of her,' he said.

Erin's eyes widened, and her heart gave a sideways lurch as she turned her head and encountered Eamon's amused emerald gaze.

'Come on out, Dr Taylor,' he said with a knowing smile. 'I'd like you to meet my youngest sister.'

His *sister*? Erin felt her colour rise to the roots of her hair as she peeled herself away from the pantry door. She squared her shoulders with what little pride she had left, and, sliding the doors fully open, walked out onto the balcony.

'Dr Taylor, this is my sister Stephanie,' he said. 'Steph, this is Dr Taylor.'

Erin put out her hand to the young girl. 'Nice to meet you. But please call me Erin.'

Stephanie beamed and shook Erin's hand vigorously. 'Lovely to meet you too, Erin. I've been hearing all about you.'

Erin shot a telling glance in Eamon's direction. 'Yes,' she said. 'So have I.'

Eamon gave her an enigmatic smile. 'Would you like to join us for dinner?' he asked. 'Steph's cooking. I'm pretty sure she won't poison you.'

Stephanie gave him a mock scowl before she turned back to Erin. 'Oh yes, please do join us,' she said. 'I'm doing a hospitality course. I'm trying out my recipes on Eamon. I've brought heaps of ingredients, so there's no shortage of food.'

Erin took a step backwards. 'I don't want to intrude on a family get-together or anything.'

'It's not a family get-together,' Stephanie assured her. 'If it was I would warn you to bring earplugs, right, Eamon?' She shone her winning smile at her big brother.

Eamon grinned back and playfully ruffled Stephanie's hair. 'They don't make earplugs thick enough to block out the Chapman sisters.' He turned his gaze to Erin. 'When the three of them are together, they make a heavy-metal band sound like muzak.'

Erin moved her lips in what was almost a smile. 'It must be lovely to have siblings.'

'Are you an only child?' Stephanie asked.

'Um…yes,' Erin said, conscious of Eamon's steady, watchful gaze.

'I used to long to be an only child,' Stephanie said musingly. 'All that attention, all those presents, not having to share anything and no hand-me-downs.'

'You haven't worn a hand-me-down in your life,' Eamon commented wryly.

Stephanie pouted and gave her brother a playful punch on the arm as she moved past. 'I'm going to check on dinner. Go and open the door for Erin or, better still, lift her over the partition. I'll open some wine for us.'

'How about it, Dr Taylor?' he asked with that same unreadable smile playing about his mouth. 'Do you want to come in the front door or over the balcony?'

Erin ran her tongue over her lips. The thought of those strong brown arms helping her over the partition was a lot more tempting than she wanted to admit. Her mind began to race with images of him lifting her off her feet, holding her against his rock-hard abdomen; the heat of his body seeping through her lightweight clothing. 'Er…I need to freshen up,' she said, brushing an imaginary strand of hair away from her face. 'I'll be five minutes or so.'

His gaze held hers for a nanosecond longer than she could comfortably handle. 'It's a date.'

Erin rummaged through her wardrobe impatiently, tossing clothes on the bed only to toss them to one side in frustration. When was the last time she had bought something new, for pity's sake? She had seen the casual but elegant clothing Eamon's sister was wearing; each piece had probably cost more than her entire wardrobe. She had taught herself to be frugal over the years. She'd had to ignore fashion trends during her teens; it had been enough to get food in her stomach, and even then it had been pretty hit-and-miss. Even now she had money she still wasn't really into the whole shopping thing. She felt too self-conscious; a part of her was frightened she would choose something too young for her, or tarty, like her mother always did.

Erin kept things plain and simple but there were times, especially like these, when she longed to feel more at home with her body, confident enough to wear close-fitting and feminine clothes like other women her age. She was lucky to be naturally slim, and she exercised regularly for the stress relief it gave her. But drawing attention to herself was something she wasn't used to doing; if anything, she did the opposite. Could she break a lifetime habit even if she wanted to?

In the end she settled for basic black: trousers and a shirt, which were both chain-store but comfortable. And, rather than pull her hair back tightly, she scooped it up in a looser style, letting a few strands fall about her face to give her a softer, more feminine look. She managed to eke the last contents of a wand of mascara over her lashes, and, with a smear of lipgloss and a quick spray of her only perfume, she gave Molly a wish-me-luck pat and left.

Eamon opened the door to her soft knock. 'Hi, glad you could make it,' he said, sweeping an assessing gaze over her.

She stepped over the threshold, carrying her keys and a box of chocolates. 'Something smells nice,' she said, handing him the chocolates. 'I'm sorry, I didn't have a bottle of wine in the cupboard.'

'These are great,' he said, taking them from her.

She shifted her weight. 'I didn't buy them,' she confessed. 'A patient gave them to me.'

'Male or female?'

'Male.'

He lifted his brows. 'Your bedside manner can't be all that bad, then.'

She gave him a dry look. 'When you're an eighty-nine-year-old widower who has lived alone for twenty-odd years and dying of prostate cancer, I guess anyone who stands by the bed is going to make an impression.'

Eamon smiled. 'You're being too hard on yourself, Dr Taylor.'

'What's with the formality, Eamon?' Stephanie asked as she poked her head around the door of the kitchen. 'Call her Erin, for goodness' sake. It's such a cool name, unlike Steph-an-ie.' She dragged out the syllables with a roll of her eyes.

'I think it's a lovely name,' Erin said. 'But do you prefer it shortened to Steph?'

'Friends and family call me that, so that would be cool if you do too,' Steph said. 'Hey, bro, can you find me the garlic crusher?'

'Do I have one?' Eamon asked, looking somewhat bewildered.

Erin watched the interplay between Eamon and his youngest sister and felt an ache deep inside for what she had missed out on in not having had a family unit to grow up in. There was an ease about Eamon and his sister, a companionship and camaraderie that was unlike anything she had experienced. Steph obviously adored her big brother and Eamon, although his manner at times was teasing, was clearly protective and very proud of her.

'One garlic crusher.' After rattling through several drawers, Eamon handed it to his sister like a surgical implement.

'Good boy. Now, pour Erin a glass of wine and take

her into the lounge,' Steph directed. 'Oh, and don't talk about work!'

Eamon winked at Erin as he scooped up two glasses and a bottle of wine from the bench. 'Come on,' he said. 'We're better out of the way, believe me.'

Erin followed him into the lounge area, which was larger than hers. The decor was minimalist but stylish, reminding her yet again of the different worlds they had come from.

'So,' he said, handing her a wineglass. 'If not work, what shall we talk about?'

Erin took the glass, carefully avoiding his fingers as she did so. 'I don't know…hobbies?'

'Do you have any?'

She cradled her glass in both hands. 'I read.'

'What do you read?'

'Books.'

He gave her a droll look. 'What genre or genres do you like?'

Erin felt her face grow warm. 'I like…er…fantasy.'

'Interesting.'

'What about you?' she asked, trying not to appear flustered by his proximity. 'What do you like to read?'

'Biographies, history, science; that sort of thing,' he answered. 'My sisters are always at me to read other genres but I really like reading for information, not necessarily for entertainment.'

A silence hung in the air for a moment.

'What do you do in your spare time besides reading?' Eamon asked.

'I work out a little. I have a treadmill.'

'Handy.'

'Yes, I don't like running or walking in the dark,' she

said. 'I guess that would be one of the benefits of having a dog.'

He smiled lopsidedly. 'I can't quite see Molly defending you from a would-be assailant, but then again I could be wrong.'

She took a sip of her wine. 'I hope you won't let slip that I have her—I mean with the body corporate,' she said. 'I like coming home to her after a tough day. It…it helps.'

Eamon watched as she perched on the edge of the nearest sofa, her wineglass cupped in her hands, her eyes not quite making the distance to his. 'I guess goldfish are not quite the same thing, are they?' he said.

Her brown eyes meshed with his. 'No, they're not.'

Another silence slipped past.

Eamon felt that delicious tug deep in his groin again. He felt it just about every time she looked at him. It was like a direct charge of electricity, zapping him to throbbing awareness. Their rather stilted exchange masked a simmering tension just beneath the surface. He could sense it in the way she held herself, the way her eyes flicked away from his as if she was frightened he would see more than she wanted him to see. He had enjoyed watching her eavesdropping. It had made him realise she did give a damn about what people thought, even though she strenuously denied it. Her face had been so expressive, full of pique, outrage and anger, that it made him all the more determined to get under her guard.

He looked at her mouth, the soft pillow of it looking so very tempting as she sat there sipping occasionally at her wine. He watched the up-and-down movement of her slim throat as she swallowed, and the hesitant sweep of her tongue across her lips. His stomach clenched low and deep with the thought of her doing the same to him.

He felt his body swell inside his jeans, the rush of blood that he couldn't control even if he wanted to. God, the thought of slipping into her, having her clutch at him with her tight little body, was making his head spin. He wondered if she would be as hesitant and ill at ease in bed as she appeared in company. Or would she be all hungry tigress, scratching and clawing at him in ravenous need?

She suddenly looked up and locked gazes with him; the air in the room tightened like fencing-wire being strained.

Eamon felt the drum of his blood kicking in his veins, a roaring rush that drove every thought out of his head. He knew if his little sister wasn't banging pots and pans and utensils in the room next door he might very well have closed the distance between Erin and himself and taken his chances on a kiss, as he had been tempted to do the previous evening. As if she knew where his thoughts were leading, Erin sent the tip of her tongue out over her lips, her throat rising and falling again as her eyes slowly slipped out of the reach of his.

'Gosh, it's awfully quiet in here,' Steph said as she breezed in with a plate of nibbles. 'Can't you think of anything to talk about but work?'

'If you put two doctors into a room by themselves, what else do you expect them to do?' Eamon asked, reaching for an olive and popping it into his mouth.

Steph gave him a mock-despairing look before turning her gaze to Erin. 'I hope he hasn't been boring you. He's not the greatest conversationalist in the world.'

'He wasn't boring me at all,' Erin said, wishing she could control her propensity to blush. 'We were talking about…about pets.'

Steph's eyes lit up. 'Eamon told me you had a cat.'

She perched on the arm of the sofa next to her brother, crossing one booted ankle over the other. 'So, do you have a boyfriend?'

'Stephanie May Chapman,' Eamon said warningly.

'What?' She looked at him in affront. 'I'm just making conversation.'

'It's all right,' Erin said before he could respond. 'No, I don't have a boyfriend. I don't have much of a social life at present.'

'Maybe we could set you up on a blind date or something,' Steph suggested. 'How about it, Eamon? Do you know of any suitable young men lurking around the hospital?'

He rolled his eyes as he pushed himself out of the sofa. 'Keep me out of it,' he said. 'I don't like people meddling in my affairs, and I'm sure Dr Taylor doesn't either.'

'Spoilsport.' Steph pouted. 'It's so hard for women to meet decent men these days. You could at least offer up a few suggestions.'

'I really don't need—' Erin began uncomfortably.

Steph was undaunted. 'When was the last time you went on a proper date?' she asked.

Erin pressed her lips together, thinking about it. 'Er, it was quite a while ago.'

'How long?' Steph asked.

Erin tried not to look in Eamon's direction. 'It was about seven years ago.'

Steph slapped her hands on her thighs as she looked up at Eamon, who was standing in a brooding manner near the windows. 'See? What's a young single working woman to do?'

'You seem to do all right for yourself,' Eamon pointed

out wryly. 'You're only here tonight because your latest squeeze fell through at the last minute. Remember?'

Steph gave her head a little toss as she launched off the sofa arm. 'I'm going to check on dinner and my text messages to see if he-who-shall-remain-nameless has changed his mind.'

The room was as silent as an ancient tomb once the door to the kitchen closed.

'Sorry about—' Eamon said.

'Maybe I should—' Erin spoke at the same time.

'No,' he said. 'Don't let her scare you off. She's cooked for us; we might as well enjoy it. It sure beats cheese on toast.'

Erin picked up her wine again, and the point of her index finger made a pathway through the beads of condensation around the glass. 'She's lovely…' She looked up at him. 'You're lucky to have such a loving family.'

He gave a rueful grimace. 'You do realise we're being set up, don't you?'

Erin felt a frown stitch her forehead. 'Set up for what?'

'My family constantly despairs about me not settling down,' he said. 'When my father was my age—thirty-four—he was already married and had three children. Steph was a surprise package later in life.'

He came over and topped up both their wineglasses before he continued. 'When I hopped on a plane to the UK a couple of years ago, they were convinced I'd break all their hearts by falling in love with an English rose and never come home again.'

'You clearly didn't—not come home, I mean.'

He gave her another long look before he released a slow breath. 'No. I didn't fall in love, either.'

Erin couldn't quite work out why she felt such a

flooding sense of relief at his words. 'Is it what you want to do?' she asked. 'I mean, settle down and have a family?'

He twirled the contents of his glass, took a sip and then answered. 'Yeah, I would like that. I've enjoyed my freedom as much as the next guy, but I must admit I'm a bit tired of coming home to an empty apartment after a gruelling day in A&E.'

'Maybe you should get a cat,' she suggested.

He smiled an enigmatic smile as he raised his glass back to his mouth. 'Maybe I will.'

Steph came bursting back into the room. 'Sorry, guys, but I have to dash. Last-minute change of plans. I've left everything ready for you. All you have to do is serve it once it's cooked. It should only take another twenty minutes.'

'Todd—or is it Tom?—changed his mind, huh?' Eamon asked.

Steph gave him a glowering look, but it wasn't long before a sheepish smile broke through. 'It's Todd and, yes, he did. I'm going to meet him for a drink.' She turned to Erin. 'I'm sorry about this. I hope you don't mind.'

'Of course not,' Erin said, starting to rise to her feet. 'It was nice of you to cook for your—I mean, us.'

'Don't get up,' Steph said, waving her back down. 'I know my way out. Stay here and chat to Eamon. Have a nice night.' She blew her brother a kiss and slipped out.

Erin met Eamon's amused green gaze once the front door clicked shut. 'She's so full of life,' she said. 'I feel incredibly staid and boring in comparison.'

He sat on the arm of the sofa his sister had vacated earlier. 'You're not boring,' he said. 'I find you rather intriguing as a matter of fact.'

Her brows lifted. 'You *have* been leading a quiet life.

I can assure you there is nothing interesting or intriguing about me.'

He studied her for a lengthy moment. 'Why haven't you been on a date in seven years?'

Erin glanced at the wine in her glass. 'Too busy, too tired, too hard to please.' She lifted her gaze back to his. 'I'm not into the casual-fling scene. I'm not into settling down, either.'

'You sound quite adamant about that.'

'I am.'

'Who hurt you?'

Erin felt her defences go up like a swish of rapidly unsheathed swords. She had to work hard to hold his steady gaze. Her heart gave a stomping kick against her breastbone, and her stomach clenched as if a hand had snatched at her insides. 'Why do you ask that?' she asked in her best cool and controlled tone.

He lifted one shoulder in a shrug-like movement. 'Instinct. Intuition. Gut feeling.'

'I didn't know there was such a thing as male intuition,' she said, trying to keep her expression bland and her tone even. 'I thought that was the special domain of women.'

'Let's put that to the test.' He got up from the arm of the sofa and came and sat beside her. 'What's your intuition telling you now?' he asked, pinning her with his gaze.

Erin sat very still, but the surface of the wine in her glass rippled with her underlying apprehension. Her mouth was dry and she had to moisten her lips with her tongue in order to speak, an action that his all-seeing gaze closely followed. 'Um...I get the feeling you're going to make a move on me,' she said. 'But I would strongly advise against it.'

He raised one of his brows. 'Are you warning me you'll slap my face if I do?'

'I don't believe in using violence to get a message across.'

His eyes went to her mouth for a beat or two before slowly coming back to hers. 'So, no slapping if I kiss you.' He rubbed at his jaw, the scrape of his palm across his light stubble clearly audible in the pulsing silence. 'Now, that's tempting.'

Erin swallowed. 'D-don't even think about it,' she said; her voice didn't sound strong and assured, however, but soft, hesitant and slightly breathless.

'I've been thinking about it since I ran into you when I came out of the lift.' His voice was a deep burr of sound that made the hairs on her scalp prickle with sensation.

'S-surely not.' She moistened her lips again. 'I was positively rude to you.'

His mouth tilted in a little half-smile. 'Are you apologising for that or just stating a fact?'

Erin was feeling more and more out of her depth. He was within touching distance. She could smell his clean, male scent. She could feel his body warmth. She could reach out and touch his chiselled jaw. She could reach out and run a fingertip over his lips. She could lean forward and meet his mouth halfway…

Or she could be sensible and get off the sofa.

'Don't even think about it,' he said softly, taking one of her hands before she could use it to lever herself upwards.

Erin drew in a breath, feeling it rattle all the way down into her lungs like loose change in someone's pocket. She looked down at her hand encased in his. She wondered how many lives those long, clever fingers had saved. Or how many women he had tempted into his arms and into his bed. 'This is not a good idea, Dr Chapman,' she said, still looking at the stark contrast of her lighter toned skin with his.

'What's not a good idea?' he asked in that sexy, deep baritone.

She met his gaze and then wished she hadn't. Intimate possibilities swirled around them like a heavy fog. She could so easily lose her way.

So very easily.

'You. Me. Us,' she said. 'It would never work.'

'What makes you so certain about that?' he asked. 'You've only known me a couple of days.'

'The work thing...' Her teeth savaged her lip. 'It...it always complicates things.'

His thumb began a mind-numbing stroke across the back of her hand, each lazy slide of his warm flesh against hers heating her to the core. She felt the slow melt of her resistance, and vainly tried to stop it. It would be so easy to give in to the eroticism of the moment, so easy to lap at the pool of longing, to dive beneath its rippling depths, to feel the pulse of his pounding blood within her silken cave.

'Maybe you're thinking way too much, Dr Taylor,' he said, bringing her hand up to his mouth.

Erin held her breath as she felt his lips brush against her fingertips. She felt the slight graze from his evening stubble, the brazenly intimate contact sending a shock wave of reaction through her belly and beyond. His eyes locked on hers as his mouth moved against each of her fingers in turn. She felt mesmerised by his touch. It brought such heat to her body, making it tinglingly alive. She gave a little gasp when his lips opened over her index finger, drawing its knuckle into the warm, dark, dangerously tempting cavern of his mouth. She felt the sexy rasp of his tongue as it curled around her sensitive fingertip, her senses almost exploding in response. She could hear ringing in her ears, a buzzing sound that made her wonder if she was losing control of her mind, drawn into such a whirlpool of longing that nothing else made sense.

'Damn it,' Eamon said as he released her hand and got to his feet.

Erin blinked herself back to reality. Of course he would stop this nonsense; someone had to be sensible about this. It wouldn't do to let this go any further. It was crazy to think otherwise. It was crazy to think…

'Great timing, don't you think?' he asked as he moved towards the kitchen.

Erin frowned as she realised the buzzing wasn't coming from inside her head at all. It was the oven timer telling them dinner was ready. 'Er, yes,' she said. 'I guess it is.'

'Do you know how to switch it off?' he called out from the kitchen. 'I haven't used it before. I don't want to call Steph; I'll never hear the end of it.'

She got off the sofa on legs that felt like not-quite-set jelly and made her way to the kitchen. Eamon was leaning over the oven, peering at the dials, giving her a wonderful view of his jean-clad, taut behind. She came as close as she dared, reaching past him to press the button which should have had a tiny bell symbol on it but in this case was worn away from use. 'That's the one,' she said. 'It's exactly the same model as mine next door.'

He straightened and looked down at her. 'Amazing.'

Erin shrugged. 'You would have worked it out eventually.'

'I wasn't talking about the timer.'

She drew in a shaky little breath as he came closer. She didn't step away; in a galley kitchen there wasn't anywhere to go, or so she told herself later. 'Oh?' Her voice came out like a mouse squeak.

His arms settled either side of her, his hands resting on the bench, creating a cage for her body. His eyes meshed with hers, holding her entranced as each sensually charged second pulsed by.

'So, Dr Taylor,' he said in a low, deep rumble. 'Where should we go from here?'

Erin carefully inflated her lungs but even so she felt as if a handful of thorns had gone down with the air she breathed in. 'Um, you step back. I step back. Easy. Sensible. No harm done.'

His lips curved upwards. 'You think?'

Erin didn't know what to think. Her mind seemed to have switched off several minutes ago. Her senses were on high alert, each one screaming for more of his touch. Her tongue darted out to moisten her tombstone-dry lips; her heart lurched when she saw his eyes drop to her mouth.

Time slowed, frame by frame, as his head came down, lower, lower, the warm caress of his breath skating over the surface of her lips, heating her blood to a slow boil. Her breath mingled with his, an erotic union that sent her senses reeling even further. She closed her eyes as his mouth brushed hers, like a sable brush against a precious canvas, soft, light, careful. He did it once more, just as lightly, the barely there touch making her lips tingle for more pressure.

He lifted his head a mere fraction, his eyes heavy-lidded as they tethered hers. 'How's that intuition of yours?' he asked. 'Do you reckon it's time to stop or should we risk one more kiss?'

The winds had never had so much caution thrown at them as Erin stepped up on tiptoe, her hips brushing against the rock-hard wall of his. 'Maybe just one more...' she whispered.

'Better make it a good one, then,' he said, and covered her mouth with the explosive heat and fire of his.

CHAPTER FIVE

IT WASN'T as if Erin had anything in recent memory to compare it to, but she was sure she had never been kissed quite like that before. His mouth was commanding but not too controlling, warm and moist, but not slippery and sleazy. It was experienced, exciting and erotic. It was daring and even dangerous at times when he used his tongue to call hers into a duel-like dance that had blatantly sexual overtones. She was swept away with it, the pull of attraction like an undertow around her lower body. She felt the pounding of his blood against her pelvis as his erection hardened to steel, a thrilling reminder of his potency and power, and her vulnerability to it. Her body melted into his heat, the barrier of their clothes doing nothing to detract from the sensations she was feeling.

His mouth continued its sensual assault, not once lifting, just changing position until she was breathless and dizzy with whirling sensations.

His hands left the bench, cupping her face instead, adding a touch of tenderness that was unexpected and, because of it, all the more enthralling. His tongue circled hers, gently, cajolingly, until she found a rhythm that matched his: slow and sensual, then fast and furious, backing off to pace the passion and then grinding down again with ravenous need.

Erin's lips felt swollen but she kept on kissing him, her heart thumping like a madly swinging anvil when his hands moved from her face to settle just below her ribcage. His splayed fingers were so close to her breasts, making them pulse with an ache she had never felt before. Her nipples were tight and sensitive; just the pressure of his chest against hers was enough to make every nerve ending twitch in fevered response.

His mouth softened on hers, slowing down the hectic pace as his hands gently cupped her breasts. She dared not breathe in case he stopped; the slow roll of his thumbs over her distended nipples made her head reel.

She whimpered into his mouth as he moved aside her clothing, that first touch of skin on skin making her insides quiver. His hand was warm and dry and very, very determined. She loved the feel of him exploring her softness, the way she was a perfect fit for his palm. She loved the way his fingers were slightly calloused, as if he was no stranger to physical labour. It reminded her of his arrant masculinity, of the way he was so over-whelmingly male and not for a moment ashamed of it.

His mouth hardened as he deepened his kiss; the grind of his hips against hers and the low, deep groan he gave made her skin tighten with pleasure. It was reckless and foolish to respond so wantonly but she couldn't help it. It was like trying to stop a runaway train; the momentum was gathering inexorably as each second passed.

His hands moved from her breasts and settled against her hips, pulling her against his burgeoning heat with unmistakable purpose. She felt the frantic flutter of her pulse as his body signalled its need of hers, the increasing pressure of his mouth and the sexy stab and thrust of his tongue against hers sending her into a wheelspin. Her body was slick with moisture; she could feel it pooling like warmed honey between her thighs. She had never felt such an overwhelming response; the sheer force of it took her completely by surprise. Was it her hormones raging out of control? Was it because she had not experienced red-hot passion like this before? Did she want him just because she *wanted* him? Was there no other reason than just the most basic pull of primal need to mate with someone potent, to be tamed by the leader of the pack, to be brought to sobbing submission in mind-blowing pleasure?

It was all of that and more, but it didn't mean Erin was going to give in to it. She had good reason not to. All her adult life she had fought against the instincts of the flesh, knowing how damaging they could be to one's freedom in the long run. She had seen it first-hand: the devastation of not being able to withstand temptation, the way a life could suddenly spiral out of control, never to be the same again.

She pushed her hands against Eamon's chest, fighting with herself all the way as she felt the play of hard muscle under her palms. She tightened her resolve, pulling her mouth out from under his. 'Sorry,' she said, her voice, not surprisingly, sounding husky.

'Time to stop?' he asked, still holding her by the hips.

Erin could feel the throb of his hardened flesh, so close to the achingly empty heart of her. 'Um…possibly shouldn't have started,' she said, running her tongue over her swollen lips, tasting him, tasting temptation, and only just resisting it.

He gave a chuckle of laughter that rumbled against her chest. 'Don't you like to live a little dangerously sometimes, Dr Taylor?'

She slipped out of his hold, folding her arms across her chest as she faced him. How like him to laugh at her. To make fun of her, to make light of what to her was so significant she didn't dare take it further. 'No, I don't,' she stated flatly.

'Erin...' He raked a hand through his hair in an endearing, almost boyish manner. 'Maybe I overdid it a bit. I'm sorry, but you have a very kissable mouth.'

Erin tightened her arms like whalebone stays across her body. 'There are plenty of kissable mouths you can choose from, but this one is now off-limits.'

He shook his head at her as if admonishing a small, recalcitrant child. 'You were the one who gave me the go ahead, remember?'

She summoned up a glare but it wasn't her best effort. 'One kiss, not a marathon. My lips feel bruised.'

He closed the distance between them, lifting his hand to trace the outline of her lips in a touch so gentle she could only just feel it. 'Maybe you're a little out of practice,' he said. 'When was the last time you were kissed?'

Erin felt her colour rise. Had he thought her responses clumsy and inexperienced? How embarrassing! No doubt he was used to very experienced, streetwise lovers, women who knew how to take and give pleasure. 'I don't have to answer that,' she said, stepping away from him again.

'You don't have to be ashamed of not putting it out there, Erin,' he said. 'I'm forever telling my two still-single sisters they should hold back. Men respect it, believe me. We might try it on, but deep down we don't want the woman we have a one-night stand with to end up being the mother of our children.'

Erin felt a funny sensation in the pit of her stomach as she looked at him. He would make some lucky girl a wonderful husband and father of her children. He had all the qualities that counted, and besides that he came from a rock-steady background. She knew how important good role-modelling was. She had seen the results of generational violence or addictive behaviour or both. Eamon was so lucky to have a solid foundation to build on. It made her feel the loneliness and isolation of her situation all the more acutely. 'Thanks for the morality lecture, but you've been preaching to the choir,' she said. 'I don't do one-night stands and I have no intention of having children.'

He gave her one of his thoughtful looks. 'Funny, but I didn't have you pegged as a career girl.'

'What makes you say that?' she asked, frowning at him. 'My career is very important to me. It always has been and always will be.'

He continued to hold her gaze as if he was peeling back the layers to the truth. 'If your career was so important to you, it would make sense that you would do everything in your power to enhance your chance of promotion. But word has it you've had issues with every director you've worked under. Not very wise if you want to advance your career.'

Erin pulled her lips into a tight line. 'If for once a director was hired who had less of an ego and more of a desire to bring about genuinely good outcomes for patients, I would not hesitate to follow orders.'

'I am all about good outcomes for patients,' he said. 'As to the ego, well, don't all good leaders need one in order to lead solidly and dependably?'

'Time will see,' she said with an arch look. 'So far all I've seen is great inconvenience to staff.'

His brows drew down over his eyes. 'That's rather rich coming from you, isn't it? You haven't yet attended one ward-round or information breakfast.'

She pressed her lips together before responding. 'I am under no obligation to do so when I'm on night duty.'

His frown became darker, more threatening. 'You've switched to nights?'

She raised her chin. 'I read in the document you passed around that the follow-through-care proposal didn't apply to doctors on night duty. The handover will remain as it stands, given the activity at that time of morning on the wards with the changeover of staff and breakfast and so on.'

His expression tightened, making a white-tipped nerve flicker like beating wings beneath the skin at the edge of his mouth. 'You really are determined to do things your way, aren't you?' he asked.

'My way works for me.'

'But what if it doesn't work for the patients?' he asked. 'You lose all contact with them the moment you hand them over. You've been lucky so far, Erin, but what if the next patient suffers as a result of something you missed in the primary or secondary survey?'

Erin held his challenging look although she dearly would have liked to shift her gaze from the steely probe of his. 'I am always very thorough in my assessment and management of patients.'

His eyes became more intent on hers, more focused. 'What about the pain incident Arthur Gourlay referred to? Mrs Pappas, wasn't it?'

She opened her mouth, and then closed it, thinking

carefully before she spoke. 'I know for a fact I signed for her pain-relief. I remember doing it.'

'Are you saying there are times when you *don't* remember?'

Erin heard the suspicion cleverly stitched in between each word of his question. Had Lydia Hislop spoken to him about their conversation in A&E about Mrs Fuller's follow-up pethidine shot? She liked Lydia—she was one of the few nurses she could see herself having a friendship with outside of work—but it didn't mean the nurse might not have used a private conversation to score some brownie points with the new boss. 'A&E, as you know, is a busy, often frantic place at times,' she said, choosing her words with care. 'And at those times it is a little difficult to remember every single detail— that's why the drug documentation protocol is in place.'

'That's if everyone is using it as it should be used,' he said.

She frowned. 'What are you implying? That I'm somehow not following hospital procedure?'

His penetrating eyes surveyed her for a pulsing moment. Erin felt as if she was under a powerful micro-scope. Every flaw, every chink in her armour, was being pulled apart and examined under intense scrutiny.

It worried her that she had become less meticulous due to the long hours she had worked recently. She had always set such high standards for herself. She hated thinking she might not have performed her job at maxi-mum capacity. It had been a trying time with the death of the young man the other day; her concentration might have slipped. It was understandable; there had been such a lot going on, especially with the news of a new director arriving. And now she had made herself seem even more unprofessional by responding to Eamon Chapman's kiss with such wantonness.

Sydney was a big city but the medical world was small. It would only take one person to see them together and it would be all over the hospital. She already hated the gossip the hospital fraternity generated; she hated the stupid innuendoes that people went on about once they suspected two people were involved. Besides that, she hated mixing her private life with her professional one. She liked her life in neat, ordered compartments. She didn't like blurred boundaries. It made her feel insecure. And kissing Eamon Chapman made her feel very, very insecure. He was clearly toying with her. How convenient was it for him to have her living right next door to call over to play doctors with him whenever he felt like it? And what if he was only flirting with her to get her to see things his way? Did he see her as a challenge to conquer? A trophy he had to collect to show how proficient he was at his job? If so, he was in for a bigger challenge than he realised.

'That is not what I'm implying at all,' Eamon said into the tight silence. 'I am merely saying the system is not completely foolproof.'

'I know exactly what you're implying and why.' She scooped up her purse and keys. 'I've changed my mind about dinner.'

Eamon frowned. 'Hey, wait a minute. You can't walk out just like that. Steph's gone to a lot of trouble. What am I supposed to say to her?'

She gave him a hard little glare as she opened the front door. 'Tell her she's right—you were starting to bore the hell out of me.' And before he could say another word she shut the door in his face.

CHAPTER SIX

WHEN Erin arrived for night duty A&E was already full and had been for several hours. Michelle Oliver was the senior nurse on duty, a woman she had worked with many times before. Michelle was competent and steady under pressure but the downside was that she was one of the main arteries of the hospital gossip-network.

'Well, well, well, aren't you a lucky girl?' Michelle said as soon as Erin placed her bag in the lockable drawer at the doctors' station.

Erin kept her features as blank as possible as she straightened from the drawer. 'Why is that?'

Michelle folded her arms across her chest and gave her a conspiratorial smile. 'A little bird told me you had dinner with the new director last night.'

Erin felt a muscle ticking in her cheek but fought it back under control. *What little bird?* she wondered. Or had it been the man himself? 'Dr Chapman rents the apartment next to mine,' she said. 'His sister was visiting and invited me over. But your source is wrong because I didn't stay for dinner.'

Michelle's light blue eyes twinkled. 'Word has it he's

determined to win you over to his plans for the department, it seems, by fair means or foul.'

Erin looped her stethoscope around her neck, trying to keep her expression coolly detached. 'Excuse me,' she said. 'I have patients to see.'

'There's a bet running on how long it will take him to do it,' Michelle called out after her.

Erin stopped and turned around to face the grinning nurse. 'A…a *bet*?' she asked with cold incredulity.

Michelle nodded. 'The residents and registrars set it up. You're the only one who's against the changes. There's a carton of beer riding on how long it will take Dr Chapman to get you on side.'

Erin aligned her shoulders in a rigid stance. 'Does Dr Chapman know about this bet?'

Michelle met her gaze with equanimity. 'Who do you think is providing the beer?'

Erin threw herself into seeing the line-up of patients, determined not to think about what Michelle had said, but even so whenever she had a spare moment her anger would kick in like a hot blast of fuel near dry tinder. To think Eamon Chapman was secretly reeling her in for the sake of a game, a puerile locker-room joke that would no doubt be laughed about for months on end. Each time she encountered a resident or registrar in the department, she felt as if they were sniggering behind their professional façades. How many people knew about this stupid bet? Was everyone laughing at her, like they had done in medical school after her one disastrous date?

She ricocheted with fury, determined to take Eamon Chapman on head-to-head. He was not going to make a fool of her—not professionally, and certainly not personally. Not if she could help it.

Just when Erin thought she had things more or less under control in A&E, news came in of a high-speed-motorcycle-accident victim due to arrive via ambulance within minutes. She felt the rush of adrenalin flood her system as she mentally began to prepare herself. Motorcycle accidents were often serious, especially high-speed ones. It would take all of her concentration and professional training to set aside her private issues while she dealt with a life-and-death situation. This was not the time to be ruminating over Eamon Chapman's despicable ploy to get her on side. A patient's life was about to be placed in her hands; the responsibility had never felt more daunting. Only her experience at dealing with similar situations bolstered her confidence. The staff working with her were competent, especially Michelle, and the registrar, Tom Brightman, was one who had shown great promise right from his intern days.

The doors to A&E swung open as the ambulance personnel wheeled in the male victim, the more senior officer calling out the patient's details.

'Approximately twenty-five-or-six-year-old male involved in a motorcycle accident. He was found twenty metres from the bike, which appeared to have struck a guardrail after clipping a car. He was unconscious with a GCS of seven; the helmet was badly damaged. His right thigh was angled at thirty degrees with a compound fracture—we've splinted it and bandaged it to control blood loss. His left ankle was at forty degrees and also compound, and the foot pulse is weak. His pulse was a hundred and forty and BP eighty systolic. We've put in a fourteen-gauge canula and run in two litres of saline. He's been bagged and masked with high-flow oxygen. It took fifteen minutes to stabilise him and the trip took another ten.'

'Thanks,' Erin said, donning gloves, a mask and a face shield.

The patient was on a spine board and had a Donway splint on his right leg and a blow-up splint on his left ankle. He had been fitted with a hard collar to stabilise his neck. With the staff's help they shifted the victim to a resus bed as Erin prepared to intubate him, suctioning the mouth to clear his airway.

Tom Brightman came in after being called up to the ward by the nursing staff. 'What's going on?'

Erin filled him in as she began to intubate the victim, which was proving more difficult than she had first realised, as his face was so badly injured. She felt the tension build in her body; beads of perspiration trickled down between her shoulder blades as each precious second passed. 'He's not intubatable. I'm going to do a cricothyroidotomy,' she said. 'Michelle, get me a scalpel and size-six tracheostomy tube, stat. Tom, undo that collar, but keep his neck stabilised. What's his BP?'

'Seventy systolic,' the other nurse said. 'His shock is getting worse.'

Erin stabilised the trachea with her left hand and made a transverse stab incision into the cricothyroid membrane. She lengthened the incision, then spread it open using artery forceps and inserted a size-six tracheostomy tube and connected it to the oxygen. Relief flooded her as the patient's chest inflated with each squeeze of the bag. 'We've got an airway, thank God,' she said.

'Good work.' Eamon's voice sounded from just behind her. 'I'll bag him.'

'OK.' Erin forced herself to remain focused on the patient, even though her own airway felt as if it was obstructed. Why was he here? He wasn't on night duty according to the roster pinned to the cork-board in the office.

The second nurse had already adjusted the leg splint and re-bandaged the fracture site. 'The bleeding seems under better control,' she said. 'His BP has come up to ninety systolic.'

'You'd better check his chest, Dr Taylor,' Eamon said. 'He feels hard to ventilate.'

Erin listened to the patient's chest. There was good air-entry on the left but none on the right, which was hyper-resonant to percussion. There was bony crepitus all over the right chest. 'I'll check his trachea before you put the collar back on, Tom,' she said to the registrar. 'His neck veins are elevated. He's got a right tension pneumothorax. Michelle, get me a couple of fourteen-gauge cannulas.'

'If you want to switch places I can do that right tension,' Eamon said.

For a split second Erin wondered if he wasn't confident she was up to the task. Had he somehow guessed how stressed she felt? She thought she had masked her feelings well. Her emotions were on lock-down; she couldn't afford to think about this young man's parents or family waiting outside. She couldn't bear to think about facing them if he didn't make it. She had done it many times; she had walked the seemingly endless corridor time and time again, facing human devastation at its worst. Raw emotion; people gutted by the dreadful pain of loss. She had never got used to it; she wondered if she ever would.

'Dr Taylor?'

Erin met his gaze with gritty determination. 'It's fine,' she said in a clipped tone. 'I've done heaps of these.'

She proceeded to do a right-needle thoracocentesis in the second intercostal space. There was a distinctive hissing sound as the trapped air was released.

'That's it,' Eamon said. 'His ventilation's improved markedly. What's his pulse and BP?'

'Pulse one hundred, BP one hundred. I've got pulse oximetry on. Sats are ninety percent,' the nurse said.

'OK, we've got airway and breathing sorted for the moment. I'll take blood for path and cross-match, and we'll start a couple of units of O-negative. Dr Chapman, can you do GCS? Michelle, get these clothes off for full exposure, then set up for catheterisation and an NG tube,' Erin instructed, remaining in control of the resus.

After completing the secondary survey, Erin spoke to the general, orthopaedic and neurosurgical registrars, organised a head-to-toe CT scan once she was sure the hypovolaemia was managed and stable, and then formally handed the patient over to the general surgical team for definitive management.

Erin stripped off her gloves and bloody gown and placed them in the bin. She felt a wave of exhaustion swamp her as she washed her hands at the sink. Every bone ached with tiredness and strain. She was running on empty, and she still had six hours left on her shift. It was a depressing thought that this was night one of five. What had she been thinking?

'Dr Taylor.' Eamon put down the patient's notes he was flipping through at the doctors' station when Erin came back from the bathroom. 'Can I have a quick word?'

Her brown eyes flickered with something. 'I still have patients waiting,' she said, shifting her gaze slightly.

'I just checked, and you're due for a half-hour break,'

he said. 'Besides, Tom's a good registrar. He's quite capable of holding the fort for a few minutes. There's nothing urgent in there. I've already checked with the triage nurse.'

A second or two passed in silence.

'All right,' she said, still with that off-centre, guarded look.

He led the way to his office, aware of her stiff carriage—such a change from last night when she had been like a warm kitten in his arms, until she had slammed the door in his face after he'd pressed too many of her buttons. He hadn't been able to sleep for thinking about her, for wanting her. His body had throbbed for hours with the memory of holding her against him. He couldn't remember a time when he had been more turned on. Although it had been a while since he'd been intimate with anyone, he was a normal, red-blooded male in the prime of his life. He enjoyed the physicality of sex; he had never sought more than that with previous partners, but something about Erin Taylor made him want more. He hadn't worked out if it was because she was more of a challenge than most, or whether it was something more elemental. All he knew was he wanted to taste that soft mouth again, to feel her in his arms responding the way she had the night before.

He closed the door once they were both inside his office. Erin was standing with her arms folded across her body as if it was cold. 'I should apologise for last night,' he said. 'Things didn't exactly go according to plan.'

Her eyes hardened like brittle toffee. 'No, obviously not.'

Eamon closed the distance until he was standing just

in front of her, not touching, but close enough to smell her light, feminine fragrance. 'What's going on?'

Her chin came up. 'Why don't you tell me?'

A frown pulled at his brow. 'You seem a little uptight. I've apologised for last night, but for most of the evening I thought we were getting on just fine. I even considered that we might start seeing each other a little more regularly, or at least that was the impression I got from you until you stormed out.'

Her mouth tightened. 'Sorry. I don't think that's a good idea.'

'What changed your mind?'

Her eyes glittered with sparks of anger. 'A case of beer has changed my mind.'

His frown deepened. 'What?'

She rolled her eyes in disdain. 'Oh, come on, Dr Chapman, surely you don't need me to spell it out for you? I know about the bet.'

Eamon felt like scratching his head. Had he missed something somewhere? 'A bet? What bet? What are you talking about?'

She put her hands on her slim hips, in a pose that reminded him of his mother telling him in no uncertain terms what would happen if he didn't do his homework when he was about ten. 'The residents and registrars,' she said tightly. 'Apparently you are supplying the prize.'

Eamon raked his hand through his hair. 'Who told you that?' he asked.

Her eyes glittered with lightning flashes of anger. 'It doesn't matter who told me. Is it true?'

'Of course it's not true,' he said. 'I don't know anything about a bet. What's it about?'

She was still glaring at him. 'The bet on how long it

would take you to get me to agree to your plans for the department. That's what last night was all about, wasn't it? The softening-up approach: a little flirtatious dinner by candlelight, a kiss or two to make me let my guard down. And then, hey presto, the one-and-only offsider finally capitulates and you punch your fist in the air in victory.' She stabbed a fingertip on his sternum. 'What a pity it didn't work, Dr Chapman.'

Eamon snagged her hand before she could pull away. 'Hey, wait a minute,' he said. 'I don't know anything about this.'

Her expression was livid as she tugged against his hold. 'Michelle Oliver told me all about it. And, let me tell you, if she knows then everyone knows. She also knew I was at your flat last night. How on earth would she know that unless you told her or someone else on staff?'

Eamon let out a long, low sigh as he let her hand go. 'I think I know how she might have found out about that.'

She cocked her brows expectantly, her hands on her hips in a combative pose. 'Well?'

He shoved his hand through his hair once more. 'I ran into Sherrie Mason earlier today—you know, the nurse I introduced to you when we were having coffee the other day?'

'Your ex-but-still-best-friends girlfriend?' she said with a sarcastic edge to her voice.

Eamon flattened his mouth. 'Sherrie goes to the same gym as Steph. Steph obviously said something, as Sherrie asked me this morning how my dinner-date with you went.'

She glowered at him. 'What did you say? That you got to work on me with a few kisses before I saw through your seduction plan and left?'

'Look, I realise this is exactly what you wanted to avoid—and me too, if it comes to that,' he said. 'I don't like people speculating on my private life, but sometimes it's unavoidable.'

She flashed him another fiery glare. 'If you don't call off that stupid bet, I will resign without notice.'

Eamon took a moment to compose himself. The department was short-staffed as it was. Erin was one of the best A&E doctors he had seen. Her competence dealing with the motorcycle-accident victim showed just how valuable a part of the team she was. She was clear and concise in her directions, and she had handled the drama with enviable calm. The last thing he wanted was for her to storm out during his first week on the job, and not just for professional reasons.

'I'll have a word with the residents and registrars,' he said. 'I'm sure it's just one of those things that got blown out to be more than it was. It was probably an offhand comment that got misconstrued.'

Her expression remained sceptical. 'Then it had better be sorted out, and quickly. I don't appreciate being the butt of puerile jokes amongst the junior staff.'

'Perhaps if you hadn't been so against working within the new guidelines none of this would have happened,' he said.

Her eyes widened in affront. 'So it's my fault, is it?'

'Don't put words in my mouth, Erin.'

She dropped her hands from her hips. 'I need to get back to the department. It's been a long shift.'

'Tell me about it,' Eamon said on a weary sigh. 'I've been here since seven-thirty this morning.'

Her expression softened a fraction. 'Why have you stayed back so long?'

He pointed to the pile of paperwork on his desk. 'I'm going through some patient records,' he said. 'It's tedious, but it needs to be done. I need to cross-check some information from the wards.'

Her eyes flicked to the papers on his desk before they came back to his. 'Is there something wrong with the records?' she asked.

'Not as far as I can tell, but then I'm nowhere near finished,' Eamon said. 'It'll take me another couple of days to get through that lot.'

She opened her mouth but then pressed her lips together, as if she'd been about to say something but had changed her mind.

'Erin, about last night…' he began.

'I'd rather not talk about it.'

'We need to talk about it.'

She averted her gaze. 'There's nothing to talk about. We had dinner. We kissed. End of—'

'Don't say it.'

Her eyes flicked back to his. 'Don't say what?'

'End of story,' he said. 'That's what you were going to say, wasn't it? You like those short, sharp, to-the-point statements, but that's not really who you are, is it, Erin? Underneath that frosty façade you put up is a very warm and very sensual young woman.'

She pursed her lips like an old-time schoolmistress, shifting them from side to side for a beat or two, but even so he could see the way her cheeks bloomed with colour. 'I should get back to finish my shift,' she mumbled.

She made a move towards the door but Eamon stalled her with a hand on her arm. 'Wait, Erin,' he said. 'There's something I want to do.'

He brought her hand up to his mouth and pressed his

lips against her stiff fingers, all the time holding her eyes with his. He felt the tension slowly ease out of her hand, her fingers finally relaxing against the curl of his.

Her eyes dipped to his mouth, hovering there for an infinitesimal moment, before coming back to his. He watched as the tip of her tongue came out in a sweeping motion, leaving a fine sheen of glistening moisture over her lips. He felt a punch-like jolt of desire deep in his groin, his blood leaping in his veins as he imagined her soft mouth pleasuring him, her tongue tasting him, stroking his length, curling around him tantalisingly before she gave him the ultimate sensual delight.

He suppressed a shiver as he brought his head down, and her soft gasp filled his mouth as it covered hers. Her lips were soft and malleable, eager to give and to receive. Her tongue met his as soon as he went in search of it, dancing around him shyly at first, and then with greater boldness. His blood hummed through his body, thickening him as he pressed against her. She melted against him, her arms snaking around his neck, her fingers tangling in the back of his hair, making him groan as he deepened the kiss.

He had never felt so totally bewitched by a woman. She was such an enigma—uptight and prickly one minute, soft and yielding to him the next. He felt as if he could never have enough of her. She tasted so sweet and yet so sexy, a heady combination that made his head spin with erotic possibilities. He wanted her so badly his body ached with it. The surging heat of his blood was like rocket fuel in his veins.

He turned her in one movement, pushing her back against his desk, his mouth going to the scented, smooth, velvet skin of her neck, his tongue tasting her before he nipped at her with his teeth in a playful little tug that evoked a whimper of pleasure from her. His hands went to her hips, holding her to his heat, relishing the feel of her so close. He brought his mouth back to hers, savouring its feminine allure, relishing in the way she responded to him so feverishly.

Her teeth nipped at his bottom lip, tugging on it before sweeping over it with the soft, moist salving glide of her tongue. He wanted to feel her skin, the silky smoothness of her breasts, the tightly budded nipples he could already feel digging into his chest. His hands went to shape her, the soft whimper of pleasure she gave thrilling him as he searched for the buttons on her shirt.

There was a knock on the door, jolting both of them upright. Eamon met Erin's wide-eyed gaze before he called out in a voice that was distinctly gravelly, 'Just a minute.'

Erin fumbled with her clothing, her breathing so ragged she felt as if she had just run a marathon with lead weights strapped on her legs. Her heart was beating madly, her mind was scrambled and her insides were quivering with unmet needs.

'Sit down and look relaxed,' Eamon instructed as he went to the door.

Erin mentally rolled her eyes. Relaxed? Who was he kidding? She had never felt more on edge in her life. Her nerves were jumping like live wires and her flesh was tingling from where he had touched her.

She sat on the chair opposite his desk and picked up a patient's file, pretending to read it while Eamon spoke with the staff member at the door over a matter to do with a patient in Intensive Care. She listened with one ear, but then her eye was drawn to the patient's name on the document in her hands: Mrs Melina Pappas. Her heart gave a little stumbling movement in her chest as her gaze went further down the page to a section where someone had circled her signature in yellow highlighter and placed a question mark right next to it…

CHAPTER SEVEN

'SORRY about that,' Eamon said, coming back to the desk. His eyes went to the document in Erin's hands, the tension in the room suddenly palpable.

'Why is my signature circled?' Erin asked, rising to her feet. 'What's going on?'

He met her flinty look without wavering. 'Nothing's going on. I am merely checking the records, as I said.'

Erin felt her heart pick up its pace. 'That's Mrs Pappas's file.'

'Yes, I know. I wanted to make sure Arthur Gourlay's accusation was dealt with quickly,' he said. 'I can find nothing in the notes to suggest anything untoward. That is your signature, I've already checked it.'

Erin compressed her lips, the lingering doubts circling in her head like a flock of pigeons looking for somewhere to perch. It made her feel uneasy to have uncertainty of any sort hanging over her. The thought of Eamon checking through the notes, studying her signature and every other detail to do with the patients she had treated, made her feel very ill at ease. What if there was a mistake? What if she had missed something? It was certainly possible. No one was perfect. No one could be one-hundred-percent focused all the time, especially in a place like A&E, where there were so many distractions as critically ill patients were ferried in and out. And then of course there was the trainee staff she had to keep an eye on, residents and interns, and even registrars at times didn't always follow directions. They were not the ones who had to take responsibility for any mistakes, however; it was the doctor who was ultimately in charge who had to step up to the plate.

'Maybe the patient just needed more than the standard dose of pain-relief,' Eamon said. 'She had a gangrenous bowel obstruction, after all, a painful condition.'

'Yes…' Her eyes fell away from his.

He took the file and placed it with the rest of folders on his desk. 'I've taken up enough of your break. You haven't even had a cup of tea.'

Erin met his eyes briefly. 'I don't want you to think that I'm the sort of person who does this…' she grimaced as she hunted for the right word '…you know, fraternises with colleagues during work time.'

He smiled as he sat on the edge of his desk, his arms loosely folded over his broad chest. 'I won't tell anyone if you don't.'

She chewed at her lip, her hand fidgeting with her ID badge. 'I feel embarrassed about what just happened.'

'The kiss thing?' he asked.

She nodded, her throat feeling tight as she swallowed. 'That and the bet thing. I'm sorry for shooting first before asking questions.'

He unfolded his arms and pushed himself off the desk, coming to stand in front of her again. He brushed her cheek with the back of his knuckles in a feather-light caress. 'Forget about it, Erin,' he said. 'I would have jumped to the same conclusion, especially given what you'd been told. But I can assure you I had absolutely nothing to do with it. I admit I want you to commit to my plans for the department, but no doubt you have your reasons for not wanting the change. My job is to find out what they are and help you overcome your doubts.'

Erin lowered her gaze from his. 'It's not that I don't care about the patients. I do. They are someone's son or daughter, mother or father, uncle or aunt, cousin or niece, nephew—whatever. I never forget that while I'm treating them. I'm always thinking of the people waiting on the other side of A&E's doors: what they're feeling, the hope, the dread and the disbelief that something terrible has happened to the person they love, that they might never be the same again, or even worse not survive.'

'I know,' he said, resting his hands on her shoulders. 'I feel that too. But that's why I'm so committed to improving the system.'

She looked up into his clear, green eyes. 'I don't want you to think I'm deliberately being obstructive. It's just that I...I don't think I have anything further to offer than initial assessment and treatment.'

'I think you're once again underestimating yourself, Erin,' he said. 'I realise you're not as comfortable as some of the others at relating to the patients and their relatives, but that is a skill that can be worked at over time.'

'I've never been a people person,' she said. 'I like my own company.'

'You seemed to enjoy mine a few minutes ago,' he said with a wry smile.

Erin gave him a look of mild reproach. 'Yes, well, you do have a rather persuasive manner about you at times.'

He grinned at her again. 'Just you wait until I really lay on the charm. You won't know what hit you.'

Erin tried to suppress a little bubble of excitement that rose in her, but even so it was impossible to ignore the flutter of her pulse at his words. She was already floundering in an unfamiliar sea of sensual temptation. She had lost her bearings the first time he'd kissed her, and each of his subsequent kisses had made her cling to him like a raft. She had never experienced anything like it before. Her response to him was so out of character. She had certainly been attracted to the occasional man in the past, but only in a passing manner. She had never been in love. She wasn't sure if she had the capacity to allow someone to get that close to her. If they did, and then abandoned her, she knew she would be devastated, just as devastated as she had been each time her mother had let her down in the past. She had learned to rely on no one but herself. She felt safe that way.

Eamon Chapman, however, was threatening to disrupt that sense of safety. From the moment she had met him, he had challenged her. It was like fire meeting ice. She could feel herself melting a little further every time he was near her. Like right now, standing with his warm hands resting on her shoulders, his intense green eyes meshing with hers, the promise of passion in the sensual curve of his mouth. His body was half a step away from touching her from chest to thigh. If she let her breath out fully, her breasts would be almost brushing his chest.

'I'm not sure this is what I need right now,' she said, unable to hold his gaze in case her eyes belied her words. 'Maybe it's not what either of us need at this point. You have an important job to do. I don't want to distract you from it. I don't want to be distracted from my work, either.'

He seemed to wait a beat or two before he spoke, his eyes steadily holding hers. 'Erin, how would you feel about looking at my suggestions for the department on neutral ground?'

She looked at him warily. 'What do you mean?'

'There's a meeting being held this Saturday in the Southern Highlands,' he said. 'It's a one-day conference I've organised for A&E specialists in the area on follow-through care. You might have seen it advertised in the doctors' room. I want you to think about coming. You might find it more useful than the breakfast meetings here. I've invited a couple of specialists from interstate to speak on how their departments have coped with the changes so far.'

She drew her bottom lip into her mouth, holding it there for a moment before she released it. 'I don't know.'

He took her hand again and gave it a gentle squeeze. 'Think about it, Erin. We could drive down together early on Saturday. I could take you to meet my parents after the conference. They're only a few kilometres away from the hotel where the meeting is being held. I have my own cottage on their property, which has two bedrooms, so you don't have to feel too crowded. It would only be for one night in any case.'

Her brown eyes eyed him narrowly. 'Why would you want me to meet your parents?'

He smiled at her. 'Isn't that what a guy does when he's seriously attracted to a girl?'

She bit her lip again. 'I don't know. I'd have to find someone to feed Molly for me.'

'If you can't find someone, you could always bring her along. My parents wouldn't mind. They love animals.'

She let out a sigh. 'Are you always so intent on getting your own way?'

He raised her chin with his fingers. 'You know something, Erin? You have a habit of pushing me away with one hand while tugging me towards you with the other.'

'I'm not even touching you,' Erin argued. 'You're the one holding me.'

He dropped his hands. 'I'm not touching you now.'

'It feels like you are,' she said without thinking.

He smiled a disarming smile. 'Now, that's really interesting, because I can still feel your lips on mine.'

Erin looked at his mouth, and her insides turned to mush all over again. He was so heart-stoppingly gorgeous. His smile could melt steel; just one look from those forest-green eyes could send her pulse soaring out of control. His body was so vitally alive, so intensely male. She could still feel his hard male contours against her softer ones. Her body was still reverberating with the pounding of his blood where he had pressed his need to hers. It made her wonder what would happen if they actually did make love. She was a trained doctor; she knew the female form, she understood sexual response. But somehow she knew making love with Eamon Chapman would be far more enthralling than anything she had felt or imagined.

But why was he pursuing her when he could have anyone he wanted? She'd seen the way the women on the staff looked at him. She had even heard some of the racy comments in the staff toilets about his physical assets. She was the last person he should be interested in, which made her wonder if he had an entirely different motive. Could she risk a relationship with him no matter what the cost?

She brought her gaze back to his. 'I guess I must be quite a novelty to someone like you.'

'Why do you say that?' he asked.

She gave a little shrug. 'I'm not able to offer you anything other than, well, you know...? An affair.'

His eyes darkened as they held hers. 'So you're considering having an affair—as you call it—with me?'

Erin disguised a little swallow. 'That's what you want, isn't it?'

He continued to hold her gaze with the mesmerising force of his. 'I would be lying if I said I wasn't interested in taking our relationship to the next level,' he said. 'You've seen and felt the evidence for yourself.'

She gave him a wry look. 'Indeed.'

He smiled as he brushed a strand of her hair back from her forehead. 'We don't have to rush into anything you're not ready for. I get the sense you're not very experienced. You can't be, if you haven't dated for seven years. But I respect that. In fact, I find it rather sweet.'

'The novelty factor.' She let out her breath on an exaggerated sigh as she lowered her eyes. 'I knew it.'

He raised her chin, locking his gaze with hers, his expression serious. 'No. Don't keep underselling yourself like that. You are a very beautiful and desirable young woman. Why do you have such low self-esteem? Has someone hurt you in the past?'

Erin moved out of his hold, hugging her arms across her middle. 'I can't help being the way I am. I've just never seen myself locked into a long-term relationship. I don't think I could handle the whole suburban thing: prams and pets, picnics on the weekend. I like my own space.'

'I'm not offering you "for ever", Erin,' he said. 'It's way too early to be thinking along those lines. I'm just talking about "for now".'

She drew in her lips as she surveyed his features. 'I can't help feeling this is more about your goals for the department than anything else. Michelle Oliver intimated as such. "By fair means or foul", she said.'

Eamon shook his head. 'No, that's not what this is about. I admit, I do want you to adopt my strategies for change, but do you see me kissing anyone else around here?'

Erin wanted to believe this was for real, that his attraction to her was just as genuine as hers for him. 'I'm just trying to be sensible about this,' she said. 'We want different things. How could a relationship between us work?'

'It will work because of what happens when we do this,' he said, placing his mouth over hers in a lingering kiss.

Erin felt her lips swell with immediate longing, and as he slowly pulled away her lips clung to his as if they never wanted to let go. She looked up at him, her heart feeling a squeezing tightness as she thought of the day when he would walk away from her and take up with someone else—someone more attractive, someone who wanted to settle down and play happy families, someone who would fit in with his well-to-do family. How would she feel if she was to run into him from time to time, like Sherrie Mason did? Could *she* see him as a friend, someone she had once dated but had moved on from without ill feelings or regret? Erin couldn't see how she would be able to do it without feeling robbed of something, without feeling insanely jealous that someone else was enjoying his kisses and his touch, experiencing his lovemaking. What was wrong with her? It wasn't as if she was prepared to offer him anything permanent. If the grapes she eventually reaped were too sour for her taste, wasn't that her problem, rather than his?

Erin's beeper sounded, fracturing the silence with its shrill pulse of urgency. She glanced down at the small screen and grimaced. 'I need to get back. There's another MVA on its way.'

When Erin got home she felt too wired for bed. She had never been particularly good at sleeping during the day. The street she lived on was relatively quiet, but in the distance she could still hear the rumble of traffic, the occasional tooting horn, or, because the hospital was only a couple of suburbs away, a police or ambulance siren. Each time a siren sounded, she would jerk upright, her heart jump-starting with adrenalin.

After she fed Molly she got on her treadmill and ran for forty minutes, enjoying the mindlessness of running nowhere. But, once she was finished and had showered and put on her pyjama bottoms and a cotton T-shirt, she still didn't feel anywhere near ready to switch off.

She drummed her fingers on the balcony rail as she watched the harbour with all its bustling activity, a restlessness consuming her that was unlike anything she had felt before. Her eyes kept wandering of their own volition to next door. She knew there was no possibility of Eamon being home at this hour. She hadn't seen his car in the car park downstairs, which meant he had left before she got home. He wouldn't have had much sleep, she thought in empathy. He had left A&E soon after the MVA victim had stabilised enough to be transferred to Intensive Care, which would have given him two hours, three at the most, to rest before he was back at the department.

She wandered back into the apartment, but just as she was about to lie down her phone began to ring from the charger on the kitchen bench. She picked it up, her spirits plummeting even further when she saw her mother's name on the caller ID. 'Mum, how are you?' she said in a toneless voice.

'Ez, I've got a big surprise for you,' Leah Taylor said.

Erin felt her spine stiffen in apprehension. 'Oh? What is it?'

'I'm here in Sydney,' Leah said in excitement. 'I got one of those cheap flights. It cost less than the taxi from the airport. I flew in first thing.'

Erin's palm moistened against the phone she was holding. 'So...where are you staying?'

'*Ez-zie!*' Her mother's voice had a whining edge of reproach to it. 'Where do you think I'm staying? With you, of course. I'm downstairs right now. I wanted to surprise you. Are you surprised?'

'Totally blown away,' Erin said flatly.

'So are you going to let me in or not?'

'Are you alone?' Erin asked.

'Yeah, I got rid of that creep Brad. He was pinching my... Er, I mean, he was cheating on me.'

Erin closed her eyes as she leant back against the pantry door. 'So how long are you going to be in Sydney?' she asked, silently dreading the answer.

'I haven't made any firm plans,' Leah said. 'Hey, are you going to open the door or what?'

Erin pushed herself away from the pantry door and reached for the security pad with dread weighing heavily in her chest. 'I'm on the fifteenth floor, apartment 1503. And don't smoke in the lift.'

When she opened the apartment door to her mother's

knock, Erin tried not to show any emotion, but inside her heart felt as if it had been seized by an artery clamp. Her mother was stick-thin; her once-chestnut hair was now bottle blonde with grey roots showing through, like the silver trail of a snail. Her skin was wrinkled beyond her years, weathered by too much sun, too many cigarettes and too many illicit substances. She was wearing black jeans that were so tight they looked like they had been sprayed on, her leopard-print top showing what would have been a cleavage if her weight was in the normal range.

Leah stepped past her into the apartment and, turning, put her bag down and placed her hand on one hip, jutting it forward like a catwalk model. 'Aren't you going to give me a hug?' she asked.

Erin closed the door. 'Sure,' she said, stepping forward and hugging her mother in an embrace that felt awkward and unnatural and heartbreakingly unfamiliar. How many times had she longed for affection as a young child and been pushed away? How many times had she cried herself to sleep at night in yet another stranger's house, not knowing where her mother was or even if she would ever come back to claim her?

'Well, then,' Leah said. 'Let me look at you.' She placed her index finger against her mouth, the rest of her fingers propped beneath her chin. 'You certainly don't do much to enhance your features, do you, Ez? What *is* that you're wearing?'

'They're called pyjamas, Mum,' Erin said, folding her arms across her chest. 'I was about to go to bed.'

Her mother's eyebrows, plucked to a single line of hair, rose. 'At this time of day? What have you been doing all night? Partying?'

Erin rolled her eyes. 'No, strange as it may seem, I've been working. I'm on night shift for the rest of the week.'

Leah plonked herself down on the sofa, swinging one broomstick-thin leg over the other. 'That's a pain, because I wanted to spend some time with you.'

'How nice of you to think of me, Mum, but you're about three decades too late.'

Leah pursed her lips. 'You don't ever give me a break, do you, Erin? You always want to blame me for everything that's not right in your life.'

Erin unfolded her arms, trying her hardest to rein in her temper, to hold back the avalanche of hurt feelings that was threatening to consume her. 'Everything is just fine in my life,' she said. 'I have a roof over my head, something other than junk food on the table, a full-time job and—'

'And a cat,' Leah cut in disparagingly.

'*And* I have a man I'm seeing.' The words spilled out before Erin could stop them. Once they were spoken she felt as if she had committed herself. It felt strange, and yet right somehow.

Leah's hair-thin brows rose again. 'Who is it? Another doctor?'

'Yes, as a matter of fact. He works at Sydney Met. He's my boss.'

'Careful, Ez,' her mother said, hunting in her handbag for cigarettes. 'You don't want to complicate your life with men who can hold something over you, like your job. Before you know it, he'll have you fired for some paltry reason when his interest in you runs out.'

Erin snatched the cigarettes out of her mother's hand. 'No smoking in my apartment,' she said. 'If you have to poison your lungs, do it outside on the balcony, but close the sliding doors.'

Leah rolled her eyes as she got off the sofa. She snatched the cigarettes back and went towards the balcony. 'God, you're such a party pooper,' she said. 'How could I have had a daughter so straight-laced?'

How could I have had a mother so unlike the mother I most needed? Erin thought with an ache deep inside her chest. 'I'm a doctor, Mum,' she said, pointedly closing the balcony doors as she joined her mother outside. 'I have to deal with the results of years of smoking. It's not a pretty sight, let me tell you.'

Leah blew a plume of smoke past Erin's right shoulder. 'You only live once, love,' she said. 'Might as well make the most of it.'

'Well, you've certainly done that,' Erin said, waving a hand in front of her face.

Leah's weathered face became pinched. 'You're so quick to judge. You don't know what it was like for me.'

Erin folded her arms again. 'Don't start, Mum, I haven't got the violin tuned.'

Leah tossed her cigarette butt down onto the balcony tiles and ground it out with the heel of her snakeskin boots, her mouth pulled so tight it looked like a drawstring purse. 'One day you'll be sorry you've treated me the way you do. One day when you're old and all alone with no one who cares about you. That's what you're going to end up like, Erin. Do you realise that? You might have a man interested in you now, but how long will that last? You don't know how to keep a man in your life. You push them away just like you push everyone away. You're incapable of loving anyone. You don't even like yourself.'

Erin stalked back inside the apartment. 'I'm going to bed. Make yourself at home.'

'I want us to become close, Erin,' her mother called after her. 'It's what I've always wanted.'

Erin sent a glance heavenwards and turned back around. She opened her mouth to fling back a stinging retort, but something in the expression on her mother's gaunt face stopped her. She blew out her breath on a sigh. 'I want that too, Mum,' she said, so softly she wasn't sure her mother even heard it. 'I want that too.'

CHAPTER EIGHT

ERIN didn't see Eamon in person for the rest of the week. He was attending a course in Melbourne on hospital management, which meant she hadn't had to worry about introducing him to her mother. He had texted her several times, reminding her about the conference on the weekend in his last one, to see if she had made up her mind about attending.

She hesitated before she texted him back with her answer. She wanted to go to show she was keen to develop her skills professionally, but the prospect of being with him for most of the weekend was a huge step for her to take. He had assured her his cottage had separate rooms, but how many kisses would it take before she was in his arms and in his bed? It wasn't that she didn't trust him—it was herself she didn't trust.

It didn't help that her mother's words had echoed in her head over the last few days. Would she end up alone and lonely unless she lived a little now? What was the harm in seeing where things with Eamon went? She was young and healthy and, after working so hard, surely deserved some fun in her life?

Erin had deliberately not mentioned to Leah that the

man she was dating was living next door. That would have been asking for the sort of complications she could well do without. She could just imagine her mother sashaying over there with a wine cask and cigarettes in hand, looking for a chance to party.

Her relationship with her mother was still on shaky ground. Erin worked hard at toning down her bitterness, and she could see Leah was making an effort not to get in the way. In any case, Leah slept late most days, and pottered about the apartment for the afternoon before going out at night. Erin didn't ask where she went or what she did. She didn't really want to know. She had laid down some ground rules: no men, no drugs. She'd had to compromise on the smoking and drinking. She knew it would be impossible to police it with her being on night duty.

Just before Erin began her last night on night duty, the receptionist in A&E informed her that a patient's relative was waiting to see her.

'I've sent her to wait for you in the counselling room,' the receptionist said. 'I thought it would be more private than the waiting room, with the patients listening in.'

Erin made her way to the small lounge-like room set up for relatives of seriously ill patients. Going in there nearly always made her feel a sense of dread. She had witnessed so much pain in there, the walls almost seemed to sag with it. When she got there the door was ajar, and when she pushed it open she found a young woman in her mid-twenties sitting there, very obviously pregnant.

'Dr Taylor?'

Erin nodded and offered her hand. 'Please don't get up,' she said. 'What can I do for you?'

'You treated my boyfriend the other day,' the young

woman said. 'Josh had a motorcycle accident. Do you remember him?'

'Of course,' Erin said, sitting on the edge of the nearest sofa. A wave of guilt washed over her as she thought about the young man. Why hadn't she gone upstairs to see how he was getting on? Wasn't that what Eamon Chapman was fighting for—the ongoing care of critically ill patients as people, not bodies on gurneys? They were people with lives, with hopes and dreams, and with people who loved them. 'I'm sorry,' she said. 'I should have gone up to the ward to see him. I've been so busy I—'

'Please don't apologise,' the young woman said. 'I'm just so grateful for what you did. Josh wouldn't be alive if it wasn't for you.'

Erin felt uncomfortable with the praise, and shifted in her seat. 'I work as part of a team,' she said. 'I can't claim any special attention for helping Josh pull through. I had some great people working with me that day.'

'Yes, I know, but Dr Chapman told me you were one of the best A&E doctors he'd ever worked with,' the woman said. 'I'm Alice, by the way.'

'I'm Erin,' Erin said. 'It was nice of Dr Chapman to say that but, really, he was just as skilled, if not more so.'

'He's been lovely to me through this ordeal,' Alice said, her hand going to her protruding belly. 'I was so scared Josh wouldn't live to see our baby being born.'

Erin swallowed, dragging her eyes away from the swollen belly. She had seen a tiny foot—or was it a hand?—move under the close-fitting garment Alice was wearing. A lump formed in her throat, dry and boulder-sized, and for some strange reason she felt like crying.

She hadn't cried in decades.

'How is he?' she asked in a hoarse-sounding voice.

'Josh is still in a coma,' Alice said. 'But the neuro-surgeon, Mr Blackwood, is confident he'll wake up in a day or so.'

Erin wondered if Ben Blackwood was being overly positive, given Alice's pregnant state. Ben was a top-notch neurosurgeon, in fact he and his lovely wife, Georgie, were two of the most highly qualified and experienced neurosurgeons in town. But they were compassionate too, and would not want to burden a distressed relative with more information than was necessary. It was important to offer whatever hope one could. 'Josh is in very good hands,' she said, feeling hopelessly inadequate.

'I have something for you.' Alice opened her large handbag and took out a neatly wrapped rectangular parcel. 'I made it myself while I was sitting by Josh's bedside over the last couple of days and nights.'

Erin took the parcel with fingers that felt almost numb. She untied the pretty pink ribbon, her thoughts going to all the birthdays when there had been no present for her, not even a card. It wasn't her thirtieth birthday for another couple of months, but she felt a thrill rush through her as if it was the first present she had ever received. She peeled away the sticky tape and unfolded the paper to find a beautifully framed piece of cross-stitch of a terrace house similar to the sort that parts of Sydney were well known for. 'I don't know what to say…' Erin traced her hands over the frame. 'It's absolutely beautiful. No one's ever made me something like this.'

Alice beamed. 'I'm so glad. I was going to bring you

chocolates or wine, but that's not something that will last. I wanted you to remember me and Josh. I know you see a lot of patients, you probably forget all the faces and names over the years, but I wanted you to know you will never be forgotten. If we have a girl we're going to call her Erin, and if we have a boy he's going to be Eamon. We haven't been told the sex. We wanted it to be a surprise.'

Erin bit the inside of her mouth. She could feel her bottom lip quivering even though she bit down until she tasted blood. The pretty terrace house blurred in front of her and she hardly realised she was crying until a tear fell like a raindrop on the little row of flowers Alice had painstakingly stitched.

Alice leaned forward placed a hand on her arm, her expression clouding with worry. 'I didn't mean to upset you.'

Erin looked at her through watery eyes. 'You haven't. It's just that I feel very honoured and very touched you've gone to so much trouble, especially when you're going through such a harrowing time.'

Alice smiled. 'You're a very special person, Dr Taylor. When Josh wakes up, would you be able to come up to Intensive Care so he can thank you in person?'

'I'll come up when I've finished my shift,' Erin promised.

When she went up to Intensive Care the following morning, Alice was sitting beside Joshua Reynolds's bed, looking at him lovingly. The ventilator hooked up to him to keep him alive until he could breathe on his own was hissing and groaning, and the various tubes and lines coming out of his body reminded Erin of how lucky he was to be still alive so far. She hadn't seen the CT of his brain, which made her feel another wave of guilt. The least she could have done was call Ben Blackwood to see how Josh was doing.

'Dr Taylor!' Alice greeted her warmly.

'Hi, Alice,' Erin said with a little smile. 'How's he doing this morning?'

'Well, he's not awake yet, but the day has only just started,' Alice said cheerfully.

Erin admired her positive attitude. It was so refreshing, and it made her feel a little more hopeful herself. She had become so jaded over the years, not allowing her hopes any ground in case she had to relinquish it later. Maybe it was her personality and not so much her background, she thought. Maybe her mother was right—maybe she didn't really like herself.

Erin looked at the chair Alice had been sitting in. 'Shouldn't you be sitting in something a little more comfortable than that?'

'It's all right; I don't want to be a nuisance.'

'You're not being a nuisance,' Erin insisted. 'I'll have a word with one of the orderlies to see if they can bring in one of the armchairs from the doctors' room.'

Within a few minutes an orderly had brought in a comfortable armchair and, after another chat, Erin left Alice to have a quick word with the senior nurse on duty about making sure Alice was provided with proper nutrition and drinks. She explained to the nurse that Alice was so devoted to Josh that she barely left his bedside.

'I'll see what we can do,' the nurse said. 'I'll have a word with the kitchen.'

'Thanks, I'd appreciate it,' Erin said. 'She's at least

five or six months pregnant and has been through a very worrying time. And it's not over yet.'

'I know,' the nurse said on a sigh. 'I just hope he makes it.'

Erin glanced back at Josh's cubicle. 'He'll make it,' she said, borrowing a little of Alice's confidence.

Erin was putting Alice's gift on the front seat of her car in the hospital car park when she saw Eamon getting out of his car a couple of spaces away.

He smiled at her as he came over. 'How are you, Erin?'

'Fine.' She self-consciously tucked a strand of her hair back, knowing how wrecked she looked from a night on duty. She already knew from her last visit to the bathroom her eyes had suitcases under them, and her skin was pale, making her freckles stand out like brown felt-marker points. 'How are you? How did the seminar in Melbourne go?'

'It was OK,' he said. 'I just flew in. I haven't even been back to the apartment.'

Great, Erin thought. He hadn't run into her mother. Yet.

'Have you had breakfast?' he asked. 'Do you fancy a quick tea and toast across the road before you go home to bed?'

Erin was far more in need of his company than the tea and toast. Just seeing him face to face made her realise how much she had missed him. He looked so gorgeous in his white shirt, red-striped tie and dark trousers with their razor-sharp creases. His eyes looked fresh and clear, his skin smooth from a recent shave and his dark hair neatly groomed. 'That would be nice,' she said, giving him a small smile.

'Of course, we'll have to risk the gossip,' he said as

he led her by the elbow across the busy street. 'By the way, I had a word to the persons involved in that bet you were telling me about.'

'Yes, I know,' she said. 'A couple of them apologised when I crossed paths on duty.'

'Good.' He shouldered open the café door, his eyes sweeping over her face. 'Hey, you look tired.'

'I hate it when people tell me that,' she said. 'It always makes me feel far more tired than I actually am.'

'I know, but five nights on duty is a tough call. ' He held out a chair for her. 'Do you find it hard to sleep during the day?'

'A bit,' she said as she sat down. 'The first day is the worst. After that I kind of get into a routine.'

The waitress came over and took their orders. Erin sat back and watched as Eamon's easy charm brought a tide of colour to the young girl's face. She knew the feeling, that heady rush of sensation at having his undivided attention. Those intense eyes with their ink-spot pupils were enough to make any woman go weak at the knees, whatever her age or marital status.

The waitress moved away and Eamon met Erin's gaze. 'So, tell me what you've been doing while I've been out of town.'

'Um…working and sleeping.'

'How's Molly?'

'She's good.'

A little silence passed.

'Steph says hello.'

'Please say hello back.'

'You haven't changed your mind about tomorrow, have you?' he asked.

Erin gave him a sheepish look. 'Only about a hundred times.'

He smiled at her. 'I knew you'd be madly thinking up excuses why you couldn't come. You'll enjoy the break from the city. And I know you'll love my parents' place.'

'Where do they live?'

'They live about five kilometres out of Bowral,' he said. 'My mother is a very keen gardener. The place is amazing at this time of year, with the autumn leaves.'

'So you didn't grow up in the city?'

'Yes and no,' he answered. 'Cloverfields was our country residence. We spent our holidays there but we had a house in the city, in Turramurra. My parents sold it when they retired and now live exclusively at Cloverfields.'

'It sounds lovely,' Erin said, thinking again of how different their backgrounds were; they couldn't have been more disparate. His family's wealth and status in the community, both city and country, was something he probably took for granted. Most of the wealthy people she knew did, they didn't have a clue how the other half lived.

'You've got a wistful look on your face,' he said.

'Have I?'

He smiled and reached for her hand. 'Did you miss me?'

Erin felt a warm sensation pool in her belly as his fingers wrapped around hers. 'A little, I guess.'

His eyes darkened as they held hers, his voice gravel-rough as he said, 'I missed you too. I wish I could have squirreled you away from work to come with me.'

Erin thought of how nice it would have been, secreted in a luxury hotel room with him: no prying eyes, no ribald jokes, no gossip and innuendo, just the two of them getting to know each other. She felt a little shiver tiptoe down her spine. What would it be like to be a normal young woman for once, to have a love affair and not agonise over when it might end?

'How about we head out of town after I've finished work this evening?' he said. 'That way we can have two nights away, not just Saturday.'

Erin hesitated as she thought about it. She couldn't remember the last time she'd had a weekend out of town. Somehow the thought of spending the weekend at her apartment with her mother was not all that exciting, and certainly not as exciting as being with Eamon. 'Er…are you sure?'

'Of course.' He released her hand, picked up his coffee and took a quick sip. 'Did you find someone to feed Molly?'

Erin cupped her tea cup in her hands. 'Actually, I do have someone who could feed her for me…'

'So it's all settled, then,' he said. 'You can go home and sleep, and once I finish work I'll quickly pack and we can get going. We might even miss most of the traffic if we're lucky.'

They walked back to the car park together, his longer stride shortening to match hers. Erin felt his broad shoulder brush against her once or twice, and as they crossed the road he cupped her elbow again in a protective manner. Her skin leapt at his touch even through the lightweight fabric of her cardigan. He stood waiting for her to drive off; the last sight of him from her rear-view mirror was him lifting his hand in a wave, a smile creasing up the corners of his eyes.

'Mum?' Erin closed the door of the apartment. She wrinkled up her nose at the smell of cigarette smoke.

Even though she had insisted her mother go out on the balcony to smoke, Leah didn't always remember to close the doors. The stale, acrid smell was starting to permeate the curtains and soft furnishings. 'Mum, are you home?' She raised her voice a little as she slid the balcony doors open to let in some fresh air.

She tossed her keys on the counter and wandered through the rest of the apartment, opening windows as she went. A feather of unease brushed the base of her spine as she checked each of the rooms. How many times during her childhood had she come home to this air of the unknown? It was like an odour in the air, a pungent premonition of something not quite right.

Erin found the note on her bedside table. It was scrawled in her mother's distinctive hand, as if a hen with a pen in its beak had pecked at the piece of paper haphazardly. She joined the dots as best she could, finally making out that her mother was going to stay with a friend for a few days. There was no address, no contact details, and no 'I love you' either.

Erin sat on her bed with a sigh, her foot banging against something that jutted out from beneath the valance. A frisson of alarm rushed like a startled gecko up her back. She stood up and dropped to her knees, her heart racing as she pulled her doctors' bag the rest of the way out from under her bed, where she kept it unless she was driving further than to and from the hospital. The bag was partially unzipped, as if someone in a hurry had not quite completed the task. Erin glanced over the airway equipment, the neatly wrapped bandages, the little packets of sutures, the stethoscope coiled like a two-headed snake, and the place where the syringes should have been but weren't.

Her eyes flashed to the drug compartment, her heart giving a knockout punch to her chest wall when she saw it was empty: no morphine, no diazepam, no adrenalin and no hydrocortisone.

She sat back on her heels and put her head in her hands. 'Oh, Mum!' she cried. 'How could you do this to me?'

'How's he doing, Alice?' Eamon asked as he visited Intensive Care towards the end of his shift.

'He squeezed my fingers!' Alice said with a rapturous smile. 'It was only slight, but it was the first time he responded to my voice. Mr Blackwood says we might be able to turn off the ventilator as soon as he shows more signs of waking up.'

'Alice, that's fabulous news,' Eamon said. 'He'll have a long road ahead in rehab, but it looks like he's going to make it. You've done a brilliant job supporting him. He's a very lucky man.'

Alice smiled. 'Dr Taylor came to see him. She got this special chair brought in for me. Wasn't that lovely of her?'

Eamon glanced at the leather chair with its comfortable padded arms and lumbar support. He felt a little hook-like sensation tug at something deep inside his chest. Erin Taylor might like doing things her way and in her time but there was no doubt she cared about the patients and, yes, even their relatives and loved ones. She just didn't like showing it. 'That was very kind of her,' he said. 'I'm sorry I didn't think of it myself.'

'That's OK.' Alice smiled. 'Are you off home now?'

'Just about.' Eamon clipped Josh's file back on the end of his bed. 'Can I get you a coffee or tea or something before I head off?'

'No, thanks, I'm fine. The nurses have been looking

after me. I think Dr Taylor might have said something to them, because they've been bringing me extra snacks when the meal trolley comes round.'

'You need to keep your strength up,' Eamon said, feeling that hitch again. 'I'll be in on Monday to see how things are going.'

Eamon gave Erin's door a knock and waited, his packed weekend bag at his feet. He felt a delicious thrill of anticipation about this weekend. He loved visiting his family, but having the shy and unworldly Erin Taylor with him was doubling his delight. He felt like a teenager going on his first date: nervous, excited and convinced he was falling in love. He laughed at himself; no, it was too soon to be talking like that. Besides, she insisted she was a career girl, and he wasn't going to marry someone who didn't want to have his kids. He wanted what his parents had: long-term love and commitment to family.

Of course, if he could get Erin to change her mind…

The door opened a sliver and half of her face peeped out. 'Hi… Look, I'm really sorry, Eamon, but I can't make it after all.'

Eamon frowned. 'Are you OK?'

'I'm fine. Well, maybe not fine. I think I'm just over-tired from night duty.'

'Open the door, Erin.'

It was a full five seconds before the door opened. He counted them. He was shocked at her appearance. Her face was pale and her eyes were red-rimmed as if she had been crying. 'Hey, sweetheart,' he said, closing the door as he stepped inside. 'What's on earth's the matter?'

She bit down on her trembling bottom lip and he

reached for her, holding her against him, his chin resting on the top of her silky head. 'You've been crying, haven't you?' he asked.

She nodded against his chest. 'Sorry, I'm not normally this emotional.'

'You're tired and all out of whack,' he said. 'What you need is a dose of my mother's cooking and nurturing.'

She pulled back from his hold and looked up at him. 'I haven't got anyone to look after Molly.' Her gaze fell away from his. 'The person I had in mind had…other plans.'

'No trouble,' he said. 'Have you got a cat-carrier thing?'

She nodded.

'Then we'll take her with us.'

A little frown creased her brow. 'I wouldn't want to put anyone out. Not everyone is a cat person and Molly sheds a lot of hair.'

'My parents love animals and they're no strangers to pet hair. Now, go and pack a bag.' He turned her in the direction of her bedroom and gave her a little pat on the behind. 'Go on. I'm not leaving without you. Oh, and have you got your doctor's bag?'

She gave him a funny look over her shoulder. 'Yes…'

'Can you bring it? I haven't had time to get one together since I got back. I don't like to drive any distance without a trauma kit.'

Erin sat back in Eamon's car a few minutes later, Molly safely and rather indignantly ensconced in her pet carrier. The traffic was heavy until they made it to the freeway, and after that it was more or less free-flowing. The further along the freeway they went, the more she felt as if by leaving the city and its fumes behind she was leaving her cares and concerns behind as well. Well, perhaps not all of them, she conceded as she thought of her mother and her new stash of narcotics. It had been an awkward moment when Eamon had asked her to bring her doctor's bag. She just hoped they wouldn't encounter anything that would need the administering of drugs. How could she explain their absence from the kit?

'What sort of music would you like to listen to?' Eamon asked.

'Um…I don't mind. What do you like to listen to?'

'Depends,' he said. 'On drives like this I like classical, but in the city I usually listen to the radio.'

'My previous neighbours—you know the ones who were in your apartment before you came?—they loved heavy metal. It was awful. I'm glad they weren't there this week while I was trying to sleep.'

Eamon sent her a smile. 'I promise you I won't play any heavy metal while I'm living next door. Anyway, my place is going to be ready in a couple of weeks, or so the contractors said. It could be longer; you know what tradesmen are like.'

Erin felt a sinking feeling in the pit of her stomach. She would only see him at work once he moved out. There would be no glimpses from the balcony, no spontaneously shared meals. He would no doubt be looking for someone to settle down with by then, someone to fill his nicely renovated house with a sweet-smelling baby or two. Erin thought of Alice waiting back at the hospital beside Josh's bedside, their tiny child growing inside her womb. She felt a fleeting sense of panic at the thought of never feeling the movement of a tiny foot or elbow inside her. No little rosebud mouth would hungrily seek her breast and no little arms would ever reach up for her.

'Is something wrong?' Eamon glanced at her again.

Erin forced her lips into a smile. 'No, of course not. I was just thinking how nice it is to get away from work.'

'Just wait until you see Cloverfields,' he said. 'You'll never want to come home, I guarantee it.'

CHAPTER NINE

Even though the sun had well and truly set by the time Eamon drove into his parents' gateway, Erin could see what a spectacular property it was as the fingernail clipping of the moon cast a magical, silvery glow over the sweeping paddocks. The tall poplar-lined driveway led the way to the large colonial house, surrounded by European trees and lush gardens.

The house was lit up with a warm, welcoming glow of lights, and as soon as Eamon tooted the horn the front door opened to reveal a couple in their early sixties, their hands linked as they waited for their son and his guest to walk up the steps. A silky-coated elderly Irish setter appeared by their side and, pricking up its ears, gave a happy bark and gingerly made its way towards Eamon.

'Hey there, Bridget,' he said, gently ruffling the dog's floppy ears.

The dog came over to Erin and licked her hand, wagging her tail in greeting. 'She likes you,' Eamon said, smiling at her.

'Darling, how wonderful to see you!' Eamon's petite mother stepped forward to hug her son tightly.

Erin watched as Eamon lifted his mother off the ground as he returned the hug. 'Hi, Mum,' he said, grinning at his father.

'G'day, son,' his father said, taking his turn to hug his son.

'Mum, Dad, I'd like you to meet a colleague of mine, Erin Taylor,' Eamon said, placing a gentle hand on the small of Erin's back. 'Erin, my parents: Henry and Grace.'

Erin shook both of his parents' hands in turn. She was struck by the warmth of their grasp and their genuinely friendly smiles as she returned their greeting shyly.

'So lovely you could make a weekend of it,' Grace said. 'Now, where is this gorgeous cat of yours? We'd better get her inside and fed. Don't worry about Bridget, she's used to cats. We have a couple who live in the barn. I found a tray and bought some kitty litter for Molly to save you the trouble.'

'That was very thoughtful of you,' Erin said.

'I'll bring her in and take our bags to the cottage,' Eamon said. 'You go in with Mum, Erin. Dad, want to give me a hand?'

'Sure,' Henry Chapman said and followed Eamon back to the car.

Erin stepped inside the country mansion with Grace. The smell of autumn roses and furniture polish was paramount; the cosy warmth of a crackling fire in the grate in the formal sitting room off the long, wide hall reminded her of many of the stately homes she had visited when she had toured England on her way home from the States a few years ago.

'I'll show you through to Eamon's cottage first, shall I?' Grace suggested. 'Then once you've settled Molly in we can have a drink before dinner.'

'That sounds lovely,' Erin said, following her through to the back of the house to where a wisteria-covered walkway led to a separate building. 'You have a beautiful home, Mrs Chapman.'

'Grace, please,' Grace said, sending her a friendly smile. 'Eamon tells me you live next door to him. I hope he's a good neighbour?'

'He's very quiet compared to my last ones,' Erin said.

Grace smiled as she opened the front door of the cottage. 'I've made up both beds in each of the bedrooms, but don't feel you have to sleep separately.'

Erin felt her cheeks grow warm. 'Er...we...there's nothing...'

'I was young once,' Grace said with a twinkle in her hazel eyes. 'I remember all too well what it was like in the early days of Henry courting me.'

She moved over to an antique wardrobe. 'Now, here are some hangers to hang up your things. There is a bathroom the other side of Eamon's room. I put the litter tray in there. I'm sorry there isn't an *en suite*. These old homesteads weren't designed for modern-day luxuries and, this being the original servants' cottage, we didn't want to spoil its authenticity with too many renovations.'

'Of course,' Erin said. 'Anyway, it's just perfect the way it is.' She swept her gaze over the white-and-grey wallpaper and sweet-smelling vase of roses on the dressing table. The bed was a double, covered in a handmade quilt following the same white-and-grey theme. There was a little writing desk under the window overlooking the paddocks at the back of the house, and a wing-chair in a matching striped fabric was set in a corner, providing a cosy nook for reading.

'Ah, here's Eamon now,' Grace said. 'I'll leave you two to get Molly acquainted with her surroundings. She's very welcome to have the run of the main house if you think she'd cope.'

'I'll see how she goes,' Erin said. 'She's never met a dog before.'

'Bridget is too old to be much of a threat,' Grace said. 'See you both in a few minutes.'

Eamon put the carrier on the floor and Erin opened it, coaxing an affronted Molly out. She eventually stalked out, giving Erin a 'how could you subject me to that?' look, before she sat and licked each of her white-socked paws in turn.

'Better show her where the conveniences are,' Eamon suggested. 'She might want to powder her nose.'

Erin couldn't help smiling. 'I'm sure she does.'

His eyes returned her smile. 'I'm going to throw my stuff in my room. I'll meet you back here in five to take you to the sitting room for drinks.'

'OK.'

Once Erin was sure Molly knew her way around, she came back to the bedroom assigned to her. She went over to the window and looked out over the moonlit paddocks; the tall trees were like sentries guarding the boundaries. The whole property reeked of family and traditions that went back over two hundred years. She could almost imagine the pioneer settlers taming the land, the sun beating down on their backs in the summer, the cold, snow-driven winds of winter no doubt reminding them of the home country.

She heard the soft knock on the open door and turned to see Eamon waiting to take her back inside the main house where her parents were waiting to have drinks before dinner. 'This is such an amazing place,' she said as he accompanied her along the wisteria walkway.

'It's great, isn't it?' he agreed. 'It's been in the family for seven generations.'

'So what happens after your parents can no longer run the place?' Erin asked. 'As the eldest and only son are you going to take over?'

He gave a loose shrug of one shoulder. 'Who knows? Maybe I'll appoint a manager like my folks did until they moved down, or maybe I'll relocate here and become a country A&E director. It all depends.'

Erin wanted to ask 'on what?' but they had reached the sitting room where his parents had laid out drinks and pre-dinner nibbles.

Within moments a glass of champagne was placed in Erin's hand. She took the sofa on the right-hand side of the fireplace. Eamon sat beside her, his parents seated opposite, and the russet-coloured dog lay in front of the fire. Erin watched as Henry slipped an arm around his wife's shoulders in a loving embrace. It was such a simple gesture, but it spoke of an enduring love that she found deeply moving.

'So when are the girls and co arriving?' Eamon asked, offering Erin the plate of nibbles his mother had passed across.

'Steph, as you know, isn't coming until Sunday. Sophie can't make it, but sends her apologies. I think there must be a new man in her life. And Kate and Simon said they should be here for afternoon tea, just after you wind up your conference. Kate will want to feed Emily first before they drive down, I expect.' Grace smiled at Erin. 'Emily is only two months old,' she explained. 'She's our first grandchild.'

'How lovely for you both,' Erin said. 'Do you get to see her often?'

'Not often enough, is it, darling?' Grace said to Henry.

'No, indeed,' Henry said. 'But then we don't want to interfere. Young parents need to find their own way of doing things, just like we did, right, Gracie?'

'Of course,' Grace said. 'But I do think young mums need a lot of practical support in those early few months. It's such a huge change, having sole responsibility for a baby, even though Simon is a wonderful father and support.'

Erin listened with one ear as the conversation moved on to other subjects, but her thoughts kept drifting back onto the subject of young mothers. She couldn't help thinking of her own mother, pregnant at the age of sixteen. Leah had told her snatches of things, like how her parents had thrown her out when she'd announced she was pregnant. But then she'd also told Erin she had slept with her first boyfriend at the age of fourteen and had smoked her first cigarette the year prior. Erin couldn't help thinking there were some things that were better left unknown.

'What about you, Erin?' Grace's voice broke through Erin's ruminations.

'I'm sorry?' Erin blinked. 'I didn't quite catch that.'

'Poor darling, you're probably exhausted,' Grace said. 'Eamon told me you've been on night shift for days on end.'

'Yes.'

'Mum was asking if you had any family living in Sydney,' Eamon said.

'No,' Erin said, mentally crossing her fingers at her little white lie. 'There's just me. My mother lives in Adelaide.' *Or, at least, that is where she is supposed to be living.*

'Oh well, perhaps she'll move across when it comes time for you to settle down and have little ones,' Grace said.

'Mum.' Eamon's voice had a hint of warning to it.

Grace gave him a guileless look before getting to her feet. 'I'll just go and check on dinner.'

Henry cleared his throat, winking at Eamon as he rose from the sofa. 'I'll give you a hand,' he said, and followed her out of the room.

Bridget the dog pricked up her ears, but gave a sigh and lay back down and closed her eyes. It was apparently too much effort to move from the comfort of the spot in front of the fire.

Eamon turned on the sofa so he was facing Erin, his expression wry. 'My mother will have you married with three kids before you can say "engagement ring".'

Erin lowered her gaze to look at the trail of bubbles rising in her glass. 'I'm sure she means well. After all, it's worked for her: a happy marriage, four happy, grown-up children and a grandchild, with no doubt more to follow.'

She felt the weight of his gaze and slowly turned to look at him. 'I'm not the only woman in the world who doesn't see that for herself,' she said.

'No, but somehow I don't think you really want to live the rest of your life alone,' he said, his gaze steady and thoughtful on hers. 'I think you want much more out of life but, because you're frightened you might not get it, you tell people the opposite so they won't feel sorry for you.'

Erin disguised the direct hit of his assessment by arching her brows and affecting a sarcastic tone. 'I didn't know you had specialised in psychoanalysis as well as emergency medicine.'

His eyes remained locked on hers. 'Why do you push everyone away, Erin?'

Her mouth tightened. 'Why do you insist on coming too close?'

'I intend to come a whole lot closer,' he said in a husky tone. 'There's something happening between us, Erin—you know there is.'

She gave a little up shrug of her shoulders. 'It'll pass one way or the other.'

He brushed his fingertips down the curve of her cheek, stopping just shy of her mouth. 'You think so?'

Erin felt the nerves in her lips jump to attention, so she sent her tongue out in an effort to settle them down.

The air seemed to tighten. The distance between their bodies was now almost no distance at all. His knee was touching the lower end of her thigh, and her mind began to run with images of their limbs entangled in the throes of passion. Her heart banged against her ribcage, huge expectant beats that made a roaring sound in her ears. Was he going to kiss her? she wondered. Here, when any second his parents could wander back in and discover them? The possibility was both thrilling and nerve-racking. She wanted him to kiss her. She wanted much more than his kisses. She wanted to feel the full-throttle force of his desire; she wanted to feel the explosion of the senses that signified the ultimate in human pleasure. She wanted to be lost to common sense, swept up in an intimate world of longing and fulfilment.

His eyes darkened immeasurably as his fingers danced over her cheek again, but this time his index finger stopped to linger over the outline of her lips, in a fainéant movement that sent a waterfall of sensation down the length of her spine. 'Do you have any idea of how much I want you?' he asked.

Her throat tightened over a dry swallow. 'This is…this is crazy,' she whispered.

His mouth tilted in a wry smile. 'Maybe, but it's a nice crazy, don't you think?'

'Actually, I stopped thinking about five minutes ago.'

'That long, huh?' The corners of his eyes crinkled in amusement. 'I should've made a move when I had the chance.'

'You can hardly make passionate love to me in your parents' sitting room,' Erin said.

His fingertip moved over her lips again. 'My parents already think we're sleeping together.'

Erin felt her face heating as she remembered his mother showing her to the cottage earlier. 'Yes, I know.'

'Don't be embarrassed.' His fingertip brushed back and forth over her bottom lip. 'They might be in their sixties, but they're quite progressive in their outlook. They met and fell in love within days. They married within six months.'

'Wow, that is fast.'

'When you know, you just know, or so they say.'

'Who are "they"?'

'Those who know.'

Erin let out a shaky little breath as his fingertip did its rounds again. 'That tickles.'

'You're very sensitive,' he said, returning his gaze to hers, holding it, searing it. 'I reckon we'll be dynamite together.'

Erin felt a power surge between her legs at his words. Her mind went on another imaginary sprint, conjuring up images of how it would be in his arms, feeling every stroke and glide of his mouth and hands, and very male body in full arousal. 'You seem pretty certain about that,' she said, working hard to keep her voice from wobbling.

His eyes smouldered. 'I am.'

'Dinner is ready!' Grace called diplomatically from the doorway.

Erin jumped up from the sofa, her face aflame.

Eamon rose with the sort of languid grace she found attractive in a man so tall. He placed his palm in the small of her back, sending another bolt of reaction through her body as he led her through to the formal room across the hall.

The dining room was a beautiful room complete with chandeliers over a long, rectangular cedar table which could seat at least twenty people. Grace had set one end of the table up with highly polished silver and what looked to Erin to be Wedgwood china and Waterford crystal. A cluster of fragrant roses was set amongst the pendulous fronds of some maidenhair fern as a centre-piece, giving the table an old-world elegance that made Erin feel she had stepped back in time.

Once Eamon had seated her, he went round to the opposite place-setting, his long legs almost touching hers beneath the table once he took his seat.

Henry was in charge of pouring the wine as Grace fussed over serving a beautifully prepared meal of locally grown beef in red wine, served with fluffy mashed potatoes, and green beans she proudly declared were home-grown.

Erin sipped at her wine as the meal progressed, mar-velling at the close, easygoing relationship Eamon enjoyed with both of his parents. For some reason it made her determination not to fall in love with him all the harder to maintain. She began to think how wonderful it would be to have a man in her life who knew how to love and respect women, a man who also respected and adored his father, the sort of role model that would give children the best possible start in life. She thought of some of the foster homes she had been in. Certainly some of the couples had been stable enough, but she had never seen this sort of love between parents and children.

Every time Eamon looked Erin's way her heart leapt, and her belly nose-dived when his feet bumped hers under the table. Those amazing eyes of his were a shade darker than his father's, relaying a secret message that made her pulse soar.

After a mouth-watering dessert of home-made lemon delicious and thick, country cream, Grace suggested they move back to the sitting room for coffee and liqueurs.

Erin was feeling the effects of the wine she had consumed at dinner, so politely declined a liqueur. She rarely drank, not just because of her mother, but because she liked to feel in control of all of her faculties. But, exchanging glances with Eamon, she realised that with or without alcohol she was not exactly in charge of anything, least of all her self-control.

The fire crackled and spat as Henry placed another log on it, the sparks shooting up the chimney like the sparks Erin felt shooting up her spine when Eamon came and sat beside her on the sofa. His arm rested on the cushions near the back of shoulders, not touching, but close enough for her to feel the magnetic force of his body. She could so easily lean her head back and rest against his arm. She could so easily turn her head and encounter his gaze, smile at him, communicate everything she was feeling bubbling up inside her. But instead she kept her eyes trained on the flames licking at the logs of wood, thinking of how the desire inside her was exactly like those long tongues of flame.

'Well,' Henry said, getting to his feet and reaching for his wife's hand. 'I think it's time we oldies left you young ones to chat while we get our beauty sleep.'

'Yes, indeed,' Grace said, slipping her arm through her husband's. 'Will you let Bridget out for a last walk, Eamon, before you go out to the cottage?'

'Sure,' he said. 'Night, Mum, Dad. Thanks for dinner. It was great.'

'Yes, thank you so much,' Erin said. 'Thank you for making me so welcome.'

'Not at all,' Grace said with a smile. 'It's lovely to have you. Don't let Eamon keep you out of bed too long.'

'I won't,' Eamon said with a teasing glint in his eyes.

Erin sat on the far end of the sofa once Eamon's parents had left.

'Come back over here,' he commanded softly.

'I'm fine where I am.'

'Frightened you mightn't be able to say no?' he asked.

Erin wondered if he knew how close to the mark he was. 'Maybe I should go to bed. It's been a long day...a long week, actually.'

He rose from the sofa and, offering her a hand, pulled her upright. 'Come with me while I let Bridget out for a walk. We can have a look at the night sky.'

Erin followed him out of the house. The sound of crickets and frogs and the distant hoot of a barn owl sounded like music to her ears. Bridget wandered off to what appeared to be her favourite patch of lawn in the middle of the circular driveway, and obediently squatted.

'It's so peaceful here,' Erin said, looking up at the black-velvet blanket of the sky with its pinholes of stars.

'Mmm, it's quite a change from the city,' Eamon agreed. 'Hey, did you see that?'

Erin leaned closer to follow the line of his pointing finger. 'What? Where? What did you see?'

'A meteor—just a small one,' he said, his shoulder brushing against hers. 'Wait a few minutes, there's bound to be another one. You'd better get a wish ready.'

She glanced up at him sceptically. 'You believe it works?'

He grinned at her. 'Why not? It's worth a try, surely?'

She looked back at the sky, her shoulders lowering on a sigh. 'I used to think some dreams and wishes would come true if I wished and dreamed hard enough, but they never did.'

'What did you wish for?' he asked after a short pause.

Erin crossed her arms over her chest, not so much because of the chill of the autumn air, but more to control the pain she felt deep inside her chest. 'I don't know. Just things.'

Bridget came back over to where they were standing, her plumy tail wagging softly. Eamon bent down and ruffled her ears. 'Maybe it's all about timing,' he said, straightening. 'When the planets are aligned, maybe your dreams will come true.'

Erin looked at him again. 'So you're a romantic, Dr Chapman, are you?'

His gaze went to her mouth. 'You'd better believe it, Dr Taylor,' he said, and covered her mouth with his.

CHAPTER TEN

ERIN had never been kissed in the moonlight before. It had a lot to recommend it, she thought as her senses went into overload. The magic of his mouth as it slowly but surely explored hers made her head feel light, and her body lost its guarded stiffness as he drew her against his hardened form. She felt the ridge of his arousal, the heat of his body shielding her from the cool night air. One of his hands cupped the nape of her neck, the other rested gently but purposefully against the base of her spine. Shivers of delight cascaded down her back, weakening her resolve even further.

After a few breathless minutes Eamon lifted his mouth off hers. 'We should go in. You're starting to shiver.'

Erin was shivering in anticipation and need, not the cold, but she felt too shy to tell him. She envied her peers, the ones who could casually do the next steps in this dating dance. They wouldn't baulk at following him to his room, slipping off their clothes and joining him in his bed. They wouldn't think twice about taking and giving pleasure. Why did she have to be so damned inhibited when all she wanted was to experience the thrill of his touch?

He lifted her chin, angling her head so the light falling from the front windows spotlighted her features. 'We don't have to take this any further right now,' he said. 'I'm OK with that. I want you, but I can wait.'

She pressed her still-tingling lips together. 'This is new territory for me.'

He brushed the pad of his thumb over her chin. 'I know it is,' he said softly. 'Take your time, sweetheart.'

Erin felt her heart swell in her chest. Most men would have been pressuring her by now, insisting on her following through on the promises communicated in the way she had returned his kisses, but because he didn't it made her want him all the more. She suddenly wasn't fighting off his desire, but the tumultuous drive of her own. It was a much harder thing to control. It was foreign to her, an unknown entity that threatened everything she had put in place to protect herself from hurt. She felt the pulse of it in her fingertips; it was like a back beat in her body, quietly keeping time until he claimed her as his.

He took her by the hand and led her back into the house. 'If you need anything during the night, just give me a shout,' he said. 'Come on, Bridget,' he called to the dog, who was sniffing around the base of a standard rose. 'Time for bed.'

Eamon saw Erin to her room in his cottage and after planting a soft-as-a-brush kiss to her mouth left to lock up the main house. She traced her lips with the point of her tongue once he had gone, tasting him, tasting the temptation she had so very nearly caved in to. She released a little sigh and, gathering up her toiletries bag, made her way to the bathroom the other side of Eamon's bedroom.

When she came out the cottage was quiet apart from

the ticking of an old carriage clock on the hall table. She went into her bedroom, where Molly was curled up on the end of the bed. Molly opened one blue eye before closing it again. The soft sound of her purring made Erin smile; at least her cat felt right at home.

The bed was soft and comfortable but it took ages for Erin to relax enough to sleep. Her body rhythms were out of sorts after her stint of night duty. She felt on edge, wired for action instead of drowsy and relaxed. She tossed and turned for a while then, reaching for the bedside lamp, rummaged in her overnight bag and retrieved a book she had brought to read. She propped herself up on pillows and began reading, but she wasn't really following the storyline.

After about an hour she tossed it aside and, throwing back the covers, she slipped on a wrap and tiptoed out to use the bathroom.

On her way back down the hall a tall, shadowy figure appeared in front of her. She put a hand up to her throat, momentarily taken by surprise, but as the moonlight poured in from the windows she could see it was Eamon.

'Can't sleep?' he asked.

She shook her head. 'I hope I didn't wake you. I've been reading for the last hour. Night duty always does this to me. It takes me another week to get back into rhythm.'

'Would you like some hot milk or something?' he asked. 'I was on my way into the house to get one in any case.'

'Couldn't you sleep either?'

He gave her a rueful look. 'How did you expect me to sleep after stirring me up in the moonlight the way you did?'

Erin felt her cheeks warming with colour. 'I'm sorry,

I didn't mean to give you the wrong impression. I'm not the sort to lead someone on and then leave them… you know…?'

He flicked her cheek with the lightest touch of his finger. 'You worry too much. Come on, let's raid the kitchen.'

Erin followed him back into the main house, suddenly feeling like a child at boarding school colluding with an inmate to have a midnight feast, although it was closer to two in the morning. The kitchen was just as cosy as the other rooms of Cloverfields. It had a large wood-fired cooker that was still burning on low. She went and stood in front of it, warming her hands as Eamon found two mugs and a pan to heat the milk.

Bridget looked up from her basket near the range but, after giving a long-drawn-out doggy sigh, put her head back down on her paws, her eyes drifting shut once more.

'She's getting old,' Eamon said, nodding towards the dog. 'She's nearly fourteen. It'll be a sad day when she passes on.'

'I can't imagine losing Molly,' she said. 'I know she's only a cat, but she's the first pet I've ever had. I didn't realise how much I would come to love her. Maybe I wouldn't have bought her if I'd known how I would feel.'

He looked at her thoughtfully. 'You can't protect yourself from deep feelings. They sort of sneak up on you when you're least expecting it.'

She looked down at her hands splayed in front of the cooker. 'I don't want to get hurt. I hate feeling vulnerable. I like to know what's going to happen and when. I need to know so I can prepare for it.'

'Life isn't like that, Erin,' he said. 'You can't always prepare for stuff. Life has a habit of throwing things out of left field. Look at Joshua Reynolds, for example. One minute his life was going along perfectly, the next it's hanging by a thread in Intensive Care.'

Erin turned from the range to look at him. 'I went to see him and his girlfriend.'

His eyes softened. 'I know. Alice told me.'

She looked away. 'It doesn't mean I agree with your plans. It's just Alice made me a gift and I felt obliged to look in on Josh's progress.'

'You really helped her, Erin,' he said. 'Not only did you save Josh's life, you really made Alice feel supported. That's what I want both patients and relatives to feel. You're more than halfway there.'

Erin sipped at her drink, conscious of him on the other side of the table watching her with that all-seeing green gaze. She had told him far more than she had told anyone about her insecurities. She couldn't imagine why she had done so. Was she falling in love with him? He had certainly turned her small, tightly contained world upside down. Here she was spending a weekend away with him in the country. Who would have thought she would have agreed to such a thing even a week ago?

She met his gaze and felt a ripple of something indefinable go through her. Her heart squeezed, her breathing intervals shortened and her throat felt dry as she saw his gaze slowly dip to her mouth.

She put her mug back down on the table and rose to her feet. 'I should try and get some sleep.'

'I'll tidy up here while you go back out to the cottage,' he said, gathering up the mugs. 'I don't want to tempt myself beyond endurance. Just knowing you're a room away is enough to have to handle.'

Erin bit her lip. 'Eamon…'

He came up to her and placed a fingertip over her lips, his eyes meshing with hers. 'Don't make this harder than it already is,' he said huskily.

She moved closer, her hips brushing against his, her arms going around his waist, holding him to her. 'I think I've changed my mind,' she said in a soft whisper. 'I want you to make love to me.' As soon as she said the words out loud, she realised how much they were true. She ached to have him hold her, to show her the passion she could feel simmering between them.

His pupils flared and his hands tightened on her hips. 'Erin, you're tired. You might regret it in the morning.'

She pushed herself closer. 'So what if I do? What harm is done? We're both adults. We can be sensible about this. It's just sex, right?'

He twisted his mouth. 'But what if it's not? What if it's something else entirely?'

She frowned. 'You mean something more serious?'

He nodded. 'I want the whole works, Erin. Not just a quick, furtive scramble under the sheets. I've done plenty of that in the past. I'm sick of it. I want to build a future, a family just like the one my parents built.'

Erin felt her shoulders stiffen as she pulled away. 'I can't promise you any of that. I told you—I don't want that sort of commitment. It's just not me.'

'What *is* you, Erin?' he asked. 'The uptight A&E doctor who ticks off everyone she meets? Or is she a lonely little girl who is frightened about getting hurt by what life might throw her way?'

Erin threw him a withering look. 'You don't know anything about me, Eamon Chapman. You think you do, but you don't.'

'I know enough to know you are hiding from life,'

he said. 'You've locked yourself up in an ivory tower where no one can reach you. Do you dislike yourself so much that you don't think you deserve a bit of happiness and stability in your life?'

His words were so close to those her mother had spoken a couple of days ago, they made her feel all the more defensive. 'I don't have to listen to this,' she said, swinging away.

'You can't run away for ever, Erin,' he called out after her. 'Eventually someone is going to get through your armour and make you see what you're throwing away.'

She threw another caustic look over her shoulder before she stalked out.

Eamon let out a rough sigh as her heard her footsteps on the path outside. 'Well,' he said, addressing the sleeping dog on the floor. 'I handled that brilliantly, didn't I?'

When Erin came through to the house the next morning breakfast was in full swing. The delicious smell of bacon drew her like a magnet, so too did the aroma of freshly baked bread and brewed coffee.

Eamon was sitting at the table next to his father, both of them with newspapers propped up in front of them. He looked up as Erin entered the room, but his expression gave nothing away. 'How did you sleep?' he asked.

'Fine…eventually,' she answered.

Grace came over with a plate of toast. 'You poor love,' she said as she set a rack of toast on the table. 'You doctors work too hard. It's no wonder you're tired all the time.'

'What time does the conference kick off?' Henry asked his son.

'It starts at nine and finishes at four,' Eamon said. 'I thought on the way back I might take Erin out to The

Gib.' He turned and addressed Erin. 'That's Mount Gibraltar. Once we get to the top there are great views over Bowral and Mittagong and the rest of the Southern Highlands.'

'It sounds like fun,' Erin said. 'I enjoy walking.'

'It's a lovely time of year to see Bowral,' Grace said, stirring her tea. 'In the late 1880s a tree-planting programme was started. There are avenues of beautiful deciduous trees and private gardens. In September there's a tulip festival in Corbett Gardens. You'll have to make sure you come down for that. Kate and Simon got married there two years ago. It was the most beautiful wedding, so romantic. I'll dig out the photos to show you later.'

Erin gave Grace a small smile. 'That would be lovely.'

Once breakfast was over Eamon led the way out to his car. The drive to the hotel where the one-day conference was being held was conducted in snatches of banal conversation. Erin got the feeling he was avoiding any mention of the night before. She was rather relieved, and quietly took in the passing scenery, content to enjoy the autumn colour and the crisp, bright morning once they ran out of things to say.

Eamon's colleagues greeted him warmly once they arrived at the conference venue, and once name tags were on and introductions carried out the day's program began. Erin watched from the back of the small conference-room as Eamon presented a PowerPoint presentation of some of the innovations that had been trialled in other hospitals he had visited whilst he was in the UK. She kept a low profile throughout the day, quietly taking in the information, listening with interest to the question and answer session at the end of the morning's session.

Lunch was a casual eat-while-you-mingle-and-chat affair. Erin was balancing a glass of orange juice and a sandwich when one of the female delegates came over and introduced herself.

'Hi, I'm Tracey Bolton,' she said. 'I trained with Eamon at Sydney University. I live in the district as a rural A& E specialist.'

'Hi, I'm Erin,' Erin said, juggling her food and drink to offer her hand.

'I think it's great you've come along to the meeting with Eamon,' Tracey said. 'I hear you're staying with him at his parents' place.'

'I'm just…we're not… I mean…'

Eamon came over at that point and stole a triangle of sandwich off Erin's plate, sending Tracey a quick, boyish grin. 'Hi, Trace, enjoying the meeting?'

'Of course,' she said, smiling back. 'It's great to see you so happy, Eamon.' She turned her smile on Erin. 'He's a great guy. I would have snatched him up myself, except his best mate got in first.'

'I've forgiven him for that,' Eamon said, still grinning. 'How is Rob?'

'He's great,' Tracey said. 'He's at home with the twins.' She smiled at Erin again. 'We have twin boys, eight months old.'

'Come on.' Eamon beckoned with his hand. 'Show us the photos. I know you're dying to.'

Tracey gave him a sheepish look, and, handing Eamon her plate—which he proceeded to steal food from—rummaged in her purse. She handed Erin a photo of beautiful blond, blue-eyed twin boys, chubby cheeked, glowing with good health, their little limbs bare and brown from the previous summer's sun. Erin felt an acute sense of loss hit her as she handed the photo back. 'They're gorgeous,' she said. 'What are their names?'

'Bryon and Bailey,' Tracey said, sighing as she looked at the photo before putting it back in her purse. 'I haven't had a decent night's sleep since they were born, but I've never been happier. And I was such a career girl, wasn't I, Eamon?'

'Yep, you sure were,' he said. 'Just shows what a good man can do to your ideals, doesn't it?'

Tracey gave him a playful poke in the ribs. 'Watch him, Erin,' she said. 'He'll have you barefoot and pregnant before you know it. The man's ruthless when it comes to getting what he wants.'

Erin felt her face light up like a furnace and buried her nose in her glass of orange juice. The conversation drifted to other topics, and within a few minutes the last session was announced and everyone began filing back into the meeting room.

Eamon held open the car door for Erin once the conference had ended. 'Do you still feel up to a walk up The Gib?' he asked.

'Sure,' Erin said. 'I need to stretch my legs. I'm not used to sitting all day.'

'Did you get much out of the sessions?' he asked once he was behind the wheel of the car.

'It was very interesting,' she said. 'I can see how follow-through has its advantages.'

'But?'

She met his quick glance. 'I have my reservations.'

'Because?'

Erin gave a shrug and looked down at her hands.

'I'm still thinking things through. I need time to adjust. I don't usually rush into things. When I do, I end up regretting it later.'

Erin felt his glance but didn't look his way. He remained silent and she was glad for it. Maybe he understood how embarrassed she was about last night and was being gracious enough to let things slide.

For now.

The climb to the top of the mountain was well worth the view. Some other walkers had already made it to the top and were busily taking photographs. Erin used the camera in her phone to take a few shots, surreptitiously capturing an image of Eamon looking out over the Southern Highlands with a look of deep concentration on his face.

'Time to go?' he asked as he came back to where she was standing.

'Thank you for bringing me here,' she said on the way down. 'I can't remember the last time I breathed in such gorgeous fresh air.'

'It's a world away from the city, isn't it?' he said, taking her hand over a rough patch of ground.

The solid grasp of his fingers sent a shiver of reaction through her flesh. How different this afternoon might have been if he had taken her up on her offer to sleep with him last night, she thought. She found it hard to look him in the eye, wondering if he thought she had come across as too easy or so pathetically desperate for physical intimacy she would sleep with the first man who showed an interest in her. The fact was she *did* want to sleep with him—not because he was interested in her, not because he was attractive and available, but because she had never felt this way before about anyone. She was so frightened of admitting to her feelings, even to herself. Love was not something she had ever trusted. Everything she had loved had been taken away from her. Why would this be any different?

Eamon was still holding her hand when they got back to the car. He began stroking the back of her fingers with his thumb as his eyes met hers. 'About last night…' he began.

Erin grimaced. 'No, please don't remind me of how appallingly I behaved. I must have been much more tired than I realised. I hope you weren't embarrassed. I'm deeply ashamed about practically throwing myself at you like that. I can't think what came over me.'

He lifted his hand to her face, brushing the back of his knuckles down the curve of her cheek in a light-as-air touch. 'You don't have to apologise. I wanted it too. I still want it. I want you, Erin. If you don't want to take things further, then fine. Maybe we should just go with this for now. No strings, no commitment, just the way you want it.'

Erin swallowed. Is that what she wanted? She was so confused. All she knew was she wanted him. She wanted to feel his arms around her, to feel his mouth on hers, to feel the pulse of his blood inside her body, to feel him move with passion to the explosive point of release and beyond. She was about to tell him so when a shrieking cry pierced the brisk morning air.

'Help! Oh God, my ankle! Oh God….'

A woman in her sixties was lying groaning on the ground near where the cars were parked, and appeared to have fallen heavily on her ankle. Her husband was trying to get her back on her feet, but she was wailing in pain. 'No! I can't get up. Stop it. Leave me. *Oh God!*'

Eamon snapped to attention. 'Quick, Erin,' he said, handing her the car keys. 'Run and get the trauma bag from the car. I'll assess the situation and call an ambulance.'

Erin came back with the emergency kit to where Eamon was doing his best to calm the woman who was now close to hysterics. The pain she was in was obvious. She was sheet-white, and when Eamon tried to examine her ankle she screamed in agony and then began to hyperventilate.

'It's all right,' Eamon said soothingly. 'We're both doctors. Just try and stay calm. It looks like you've broken your ankle. We'll do what we can to ease the pain until the ambulance arrives.'

'How far away is the ambulance?' the worried husband asked.

'About half an hour,' Eamon said. 'Apparently there was an accident on the freeway earlier. But we've got medical supplies to keep your wife in relative comfort until they get here.'

Erin felt her throat tighten in panic when Eamon turned his gaze on her.

'We'd better administer some morphine while we wait,' he said.

'Um…I don't think there's any in the kit.'

The space between his brows narrowed. 'What about some diazepam? That might take the edge off it.'

She bit her lip. 'Sorry, the drugs were past their use-by date. I…I forgot to replace them.'

He gave her another frown before turning back to the patient. Erin listened as he eventually calmed the woman down, getting her into a more comfortable position while he removed her shoe and sock in preparation for the ambulance arrival. The woman whimpered in pain while her husband hovered about helplessly.

A small crowd had gathered, which made Erin feel all the more inadequate and uncomfortable. Guilt struck at her with powerful blows. She should have known something like this would happen. She should never have left her bag in reach of her mother; it was like leaving candy out near a child. Leah Taylor just couldn't help herself. And now a poor, innocent woman was suffering unnecessarily because Erin had not had the foresight to take adequate precautions.

The wail of an ambulance had never been more welcome to Erin's ears. It seemed to be hours since Eamon had made the call, but as it happened it was only about twenty minutes. The paramedics quickly and competently took over, thanking Eamon for his help before they drove off with the patient loaded in the back and her husband following in his car.

Eamon picked up the trauma kit where Erin had placed it earlier. 'We'd better get back for dinner,' he said, leading the way to the car. 'Kate and Simon should have arrived by now.'

Erin waited until they were on their way before she spoke. 'I'm really sorry about that. I should have restocked the kit.'

'It can happen to anyone,' he said graciously, although Erin noticed there was a small frown pulling at his forehead all the way back to Cloverfields.

As soon as Eamon pulled up in front of the house a slim woman who looked like Steph but a few years older came rushing over. She barely waited until he was out of the car before she hugged him tightly. 'It's *sooo* good to see you,' she said. 'Wait until you see how much Emily has grown.'

Eamon hugged her back, before releasing her to open Erin's door. 'Katie, this is Erin. Erin, Kate, the eldest of my three sisters.'

'Hi, Erin,' Kate said with a friendly smile. 'Lovely to meet you. Steph told me how gorgeous you are.' She grinned up at her big brother. 'Well done, bro, a great improvement on the last one. I thoroughly approve.'

Erin watched as he tugged at his sister's hair as if she was five years old instead of a married woman with a two-month-old baby. Another little pang of envy assailed her at seeing how much love there was between the siblings. But when Kate's husband, Simon, came over and handed baby Emily to Eamon, Erin felt an even deeper pain-like sensation. Eamon cradled the tiny baby in his strong arms, holding her gently but competently, as if he did it every day of his life.

'Hello, gorgeous girl,' he said. 'My, you have grown. Are you keeping your mummy and daddy on their toes?'

'And then some,' Simon said with a wry smile.

Kate slipped her arm through one of Erin's. 'Come and tell me all about how you met my brother,' she said, leading the way to the house.

That evening was one of the most pleasant Erin had ever experienced. She was enveloped with the Chapman family's friendliness and warmth, her shyness gradually easing as she felt more and more at home.

One of the most poignant moments was when Kate handed Emily to her to hold while she helped Grace with something in the kitchen just before everyone was about to head off to bed. Erin sat in the sitting room with the fire crackling in the hearth, the baby cooing up at her, waving her little starfish hands about, a bubble of saliva dribbling out of her tiny rosebud mouth. Erin felt a flood of emotions wash over her as she cradled the child. This was just part of what she would be missing, she thought. Not just the experience of giving birth, but nurturing that child, watching it grow and mature, bonding with it along with its father, as Kate and Simon had so securely bonded.

Erin captured one of the little flailing hands and pressed a soft kiss to each of the tiny fingertips. The baby smiled a gummy smile, and Erin felt her chest constrict again. Had her mother ever felt like this with her? she wondered. How could she have? Within days of her birth Leah had been back on the streets looking for the drugs she craved.

'She's beautiful, isn't she?'

Erin looked up to see Eamon had come in. She had been so lost in the moment she hadn't heard him approach. 'She certainly is,' she said, looking back down at the baby, whose little eyelids were fluttering as she fought against sleep.

Eamon sat next to her on the sofa and, reaching out, brushed one of his fingertips down the baby's cheek, close to where she was cradled against Erin's breast. 'It's a pity they have to grow up so fast,' he said.

'Some have to grow up faster than others.' Erin hardly realised she had said the words out loud until she saw the way Eamon was looking at her. He had that thoughtful look on his face, as if he was trying to put the pieces of a complicated puzzle together.

'Things were pretty tough on you growing up, weren't they?' he said after a long moment.

She looked back down at the baby lying in her arms. 'It wasn't anything like your childhood, that's for sure.'

'I recognise how lucky the girls and I have been,' he said. 'It's not something I've ever taken for granted.'

Erin wanted to tell him everything; the words were hovering on her tongue, but something held her back. Pride, shame, perhaps a combination of both. Her background was so disparate from his. The experiences she'd had were unthinkable in his family context. Would his family be so welcoming to her if they knew the truth about her upbringing?

'You absolute darling!' Kate whispered as she tiptoed into the room. 'You've got her to sleep. You must have a magic touch because she doesn't usually settle for anyone but me.'

Erin carefully handed over the sleeping baby. 'She was a little angel,' she said. 'I could have sat here all night with her.'

Kate gave her a grin. 'I'll remember that at three in the morning when she wakes up and won't go back down. I'll come in search of you and hand her over.'

Kate left with the baby and Eamon turned to Erin. 'Do you fancy a nightcap?' he asked.

Erin didn't really want a drink, but she did want to prolong the evening with him. Because there had been people around all day, they hadn't had a moment by themselves. It had been so hard, seeing him but not touching him, watching his sensual mouth curved upwards in a smile but not being able to kiss it. The thought of a few stolen minutes with him now was too tempting to resist. 'That would be nice,' she said, adding after a little pause, 'I had a lovely day today. Not just at the conference but here with your parents, sister and brother-in-law, and of course little Emily. I've never met a nicer family. Everyone has been so welcoming to me, so friendly and open.'

Eamon smiled as he handed her a cognac. 'They're pretty special, aren't they? I'm glad you like them. They've certainly taken a shine to you.'

Erin dropped her gaze to the cognac glass cradled in her hands. 'Eamon, I've been doing some thinking about...' she snatched in an uneven breath '...about us.'

He took the seat next to her on the sofa, one of his arms going along the back, his fingers idly playing with her hair. 'Go on,' he prompted.

She looked at him, feeling her heart tighten as his eyes darkened with desire. 'I've never met anyone quite like you before. It's been amazing to spend time with someone who is so...' she paused to search for an adequate word '...so well-balanced.'

His fingers caressed the back of her neck in a bone-melting touch. 'I'm not perfect, Erin. I have lots of faults just like anyone else.'

She grimaced ruefully. 'Not as many as me. You're the first man who's taken the time to get to know me. I can't tell you how much that means to me.'

He sent the point of his index finger on a sensual discovery of her lips. 'I'd like to get to know you even more,' he said. 'I've been kicking myself over how I handled last night.'

'Oh?'

He brushed his thumb over her bottom lip. 'Yeah,' he said. 'I should have carried you off to bed while I had the chance. You wanted me. I wanted you. I blew it.'

'I still want you,' she said unashamedly. 'I can't believe how much I want you.' She gave him a self-deprecating look. 'I can't believe I'm even admitting it.'

He took the cognac glass out of her hand and placed it alongside his on the coffee table, his eyes smouldering as they came back to mesh with hers. 'Not here. I want us to be alone, totally alone. So, how about it? Tomorrow night. My apartment. My bed. A date?'

Erin felt her belly flip over as his head came down. 'It's a date,' she whispered as his mouth covered hers.

CHAPTER ELEVEN

THE drive back to Sydney the following afternoon was full of simmering tension. Erin could feel the anticipation building in her body. It had been building all day. Each time Eamon caught her glance, she felt a hot spurt of longing fill her; every time he brushed against her or linked his fingers with hers she would feel as if her bones had liquefied. She wondered if that was why he hadn't taken her to his room the night before, to ramp up her desire for him so she would have no second thoughts later tonight once they were alone in his apartment. He had kissed her for endless minutes on the sofa, he had kissed her outside her bedroom door, but then he had stopped.

And it had worked.

For now all she could think of was finally being alone with him, to feel his skin under her fingers, to explore every plane and contour of his body with her hands and her mouth.

By the time he drove into the apartment car park Erin's heart was beating like a drum. The journey up in the lift made her pulse soar, the extra time it took to deposit Molly next door stretching out the tension to snapping point. The air vibrated with it when Eamon opened his apartment door for her to pass through, his eyes dark with promise.

Erin barely waited for him to close the door. She fisted a hand in the front of his shirt at the same time his head came down, his mouth crushing hers beneath the passionate pressure of his.

This was no tender, tentatively exploring kiss. This was a kiss that stated implacably what was going to happen next. Flames of need flashed through Erin's veins as he backed her further into the room, almost toppling a lamp on the way.

'God, I nearly went crazy back there,' Eamon said, breathing heavily.

'Back where?' Erin asked, planting a hot, moist kiss to his neck.

He nibbled at her earlobe, his low, deep voice sending shivers through her. 'At Cloverfields. In the car. In the lift. All of it. I couldn't wait to get back here and do this…'

Erin gasped as he worked at her clothes, removing them with heart-stopping deftness until she was in nothing but her bra and knickers. She fumbled with his shirt buttons, but in the end he shrugged it off without undoing the last ones.

He lifted her in one effortless movement and carried her into his bedroom, sliding her down his body, making her feel his arousal all the way. 'Tell me to slow down,' he said in a ragged tone.

'I don't want you to slow down,' she said as she went for his belt.

She heard him suck in a breath as she slid the belt out of his trousers, her fingers lightly skating over him before she lowered his zip. She was going on instinct, taking her cue from his reaction; the thrill of feeling the satin-covered steel of him in her hand was breathtaking.

He pulled her hand away when he could take her caresses no more, pushing her back on the bed until they were a tangle of limbs and hungry, searching mouths.

Erin arched her back as he found her breasts, his mouth a hot, sweet torture as he suckled and stroked and laved in turn. He went lower to the cave of her belly button, his tongue dipping into the tiny whorl of sensitive flesh until her senses were skyrocketing. He continued on, lower and lower, his warm breath dancing over her feminine folds. What he did next lifted every hair on her scalp; the feel of his lips and tongue in such an intimate caress was almost too much for her. She whimpered and grasped at his head, not sure she could cope with the whirlpool of sensations threatening to consume her.

'It's all right,' he coaxed gently. 'Just relax and let go.'

She felt her flesh flutter with the first wave of pleasure, and then an avalanche followed. She felt the aftershocks ricochet through her, spasms of delicious feelings that made her mind empty of everything but ecstasy.

He moved back over her, his hair-roughened legs entrapping her beneath him. He reached past her right shoulder to the bedside table drawer, taking out a condom. She held her breath as he put it on, the anticipation of him finally possessing her making her heart pump with excitement.

She placed her hands on the front of his shoulders, meeting his eyes with colour flooding her face. 'Eamon, I know this is really bad timing, but...' She bit her lip before continuing, 'The thing is, I've never really done this before. Not the whole way.'

His eyes softened. 'Are you telling me you're a virgin?'

She winced in embarrassment. 'I feel like a pariah.' She put one of her hands over her eyes. 'God, how pathetic it sounds. Nearly thirty years old and never had sex.'

Eamon tugged her hand away from her face, his expression meltingly soft. 'Hey,' he said in a husky tone. 'It's nothing to be ashamed of.'

She screwed up her face. 'You don't think it's pathetic?'

He smiled and pressed a kiss to the middle of her forehead. 'I think it's the most beautiful thing that you want me to be your first. Are you sure you want to go through with it? Do you need more time to think about it?'

Erin linked her arms around his neck. 'Maybe I think too much. I worry too much about what could go wrong instead of concentrating on what is going right. This feels right.'

He kissed her again, softly, tenderly. 'It feels right for me too,' he said. 'It felt right from the moment I met you.'

Erin brought his head down and sighed with pleasure as he kissed her deeply. She knew he was working hard to pace himself; she could feel the tension in his body and the increasing urgency of his mouth as it captured hers again. His erection was against the feminine seam of her body and she opened to him instinctively, that first smooth, cautious glide of his body making her spine unhinge vertebra by vertebra. Her body tightened around him, gripping him, delighting in the feel of him moving slowly but surely within her. He was so patient with her, pausing until he was sure she was able to take him inch by inch, her body adjusting to his thickness, her senses crying out with delight at feeling his total possession. He slowly began to build his pace, his inexorable climb to the summit of release carrying her along with him. She felt her body swell and pulse with need, the inner muscles of her core hot and moist as he drove through, time and time again. Her fingers dug into his taut buttocks, the sensations building until she was writhing beneath him, swept up into another vortex of earth-shattering rapture as she felt him finally let go. She held him tightly as he shuddered, emptying himself with a low, deep groan of primal male pleasure.

'Am I too heavy for you?' he asked after his breathing had steadied a little.

'No.' Erin settled against him, her fingers playing with his hair as she looked into his eyes. 'I like the feel of you right where you are.'

'I like the feel of it too,' he said. 'You were amazing, sweetheart. You nearly blew the top of my head off.'

She smiled softly and traced his mouth with her fingertip. 'I never knew it could be like that…you know… so fulfilling. At least not the first time.'

He grabbed her finger and sucked on the end of it, holding her gaze with the burning heat of his. 'It will only get better,' he said. 'Practice makes perfect, right?'

Erin felt a playful smile tug at her mouth. 'So does that mean we get to do it again?'

His eyes darkened. 'Damn right it does,' he said and, swooping down, covered her mouth with his.

Erin felt as if she was floating when she arrived at work the following day. Her body felt so different, so alive and tingling all over after spending the night curled up in Eamon's arms. He had left early for work, and she had spent an extra half-hour lying in his bed, surrounded by the smell of him on the sheets and on her skin.

Although they had made love several times she had made no promises to him; she had said nothing to him of her feelings. She had felt too shy to confess how much and how deeply she loved him. She didn't want him to think his passionate awakening of her senses had made her fall in love with him out of a pathetic sort of gratefulness. It had started a long time before that, she just hadn't realised it at the time. The moment she had met him had been life changing. How could she have known that the tall man getting out of the lift that day would cause her to question her adamantine stance on remaining single and childless? Ever since she had seen him holding his tiny niece she had felt the stirring of deep, maternal urges within her. They had lain dormant for all this time, but it had taken that tender moment to make her realise she *did* want it all. The only question was: could she have it?

The first couple of hours of her shift in A&E were so hectic, Erin didn't have time to think about her relationship with Eamon. A cardiac arrest came in at the same time as a multi-trauma. She worked tirelessly with the staff as she carefully assessed and prioritised patients, not stopping until the last patient was taken up to Theatre.

Erin was writing up the last of the notes when Tom Brightman, the registrar, came over carrying one of the department phones. He placed his hand over the mouthpiece, his expression grim. 'Dr Taylor, it's Mr Gourlay. He says it's urgent.'

Erin inwardly groaned as she took the phone. 'Erin Taylor.'

'What the hell do you think you're doing down there in A&E?' Arthur blasted her without preamble. 'That last patient you sent up went into respiratory failure. We only just managed to salvage him.'

Erin straightened in her chair, her hand tightening around the phone. 'Mr Yates?'

'Yes, the man with the flail segment,' Arthur blustered. 'He was screaming in pain by the time he got up here.'

Erin frowned. 'Mr Yates was given pethidine on arrival. The x-rays showed five ribs broken in two places so we gave him another shot before he was taken up to Theatre. If you don't believe me, check the notes. It's written up.'

'Who gave him the injection?' Arthur asked.

Erin thought back to the pandemonium in A&E when Mr Yates had come in with his wife and daughter, all seriously injured from a motor-vehicle accident, at the same time an elderly man had come in with chest pain and had subsequently arrested. Lydia and Tom as well as two residents and an intern had worked alongside her, following her directions, bringing her equipment and performing procedures under her guidance. 'Lydia Hislop gave him the second shot,' she said. 'I gave him the first.'

'I'm having another word with the director about this incompetence,' Arthur said. 'Just about every time you're on duty patients are compromised by inadequate pain-management.'

Erin opened her mouth to defend herself but the line went dead as the surgeon hung up.

Tom gave her a look of empathy as she handed him back the phone. 'I tried to tell him we did it by the book, but he wouldn't listen,' he said.

Erin sighed as she pushed back her chair to stand. 'I'd better have a word with Dr Chapman.'

'Do you want me to have a word with Lydia?' Tom asked. 'Maybe she made a mistake or something.'

Erin shook her head. 'No way,' she said. 'Lydia is one of the most competent and switched-on nurses in this department. In any case, I saw her inject the patient.'

Tom shrugged. 'Maybe it's a problem with the batch.'

Erin looked at him for a long moment.

'What did I say?' Tom said.

'Never mind,' Erin said, moving past him. 'Keep an eye on things until I get back.'

Eamon drummed his fingers on his desk, his brow creased into a network of lines. Arthur Gourlay's accusations were still ringing in his ears. A little niggling worry kept eating at him. He didn't like where his thoughts were leading him, but as director he had a responsibility to put personal issues aside in order to make objective judgements about the level of care patients were receiving. Was it just a coincidence that Erin's trauma kit had had no drugs in it at the weekend? He physically winced as he thought about the possibility of her siphoning off narcotics for personal use. It was unthinkable…or was it? Was he allowing his feelings and attraction for her to cloud his judgement? More to the point, had *she* used his attraction to her to muddy his thinking?

The documents from the previous incident were in front of him; her signature had been verified. There was no doubt she had signed for the drugs, but the question was *had* she administered them to the patient?

He had read of this type of scenario before. There were several cases where a doctor or staff member had stolen drugs from the department for personal use.

Although strict guidelines were in place, A&E at peak times was harder than other departments to monitor. There was a lot of activity when multiple cases came in; junior staff often had to perform procedures such as injections while the more senior staff managed resus or bleeding control. Eamon had experienced the bedlam first-hand but had always been stringent in checking and double-checking the paperwork.

If only Erin wasn't so prickly and defensive. He couldn't help feeling she was hiding something, which made it even harder for him to know how to approach this sensitive situation.

There was a knock at the door, and when he issued the command to come in he felt a jolt of reaction zap him when Erin entered his office.

'Erin.' He rose to his feet. 'I was just about to call you.'

'I had to see you,' she said. 'Has Arthur Gourlay called you?'

'Yes. It seems there's been another incident of inadequate pain-relief, this time almost resulting in a death,' Eamon said gravely.

She worried at her bottom lip. 'Look, I know I should have told you earlier, but I had another incident a few days ago. I should have mentioned it when we talked about the Pappas incident, but I thought you would think… Well, I should have mentioned it regardless.'

Eamon kept his gaze steady on hers. 'Go on.'

She moistened her lips. 'I had a patient with a bowel obstruction come in—a Mrs Fuller. A&E was busy and I had a lot to keep track of. I…I looked through the notes once things had quietened down and I saw where I'd signed for a second shot of pethidine.'

'And?'

Her brow furrowed further. 'The thing is…' her throat rose and fell '…I don't remember signing for it, although it is definitely my signature.'

Eamon chose his words carefully. 'So what you are saying is you are not sure if you signed for it or not?'

She bit her lip again. 'I don't know what I'm saying. I just can't explain how patients have ended up without the pain-relief I thought we'd administered. It doesn't make sense.'

Eamon let a small silence pass. He wanted to believe her. Was he so in love with her that he couldn't be objective any more? 'Do you have any explanation for what's happened with these patients on transferral to Mr Gourlay's care?' he asked.

'Tom Brightman suggested something just before I came to see you,' she said. 'He said maybe something was wrong with the batch of pethidine.'

'If so then why are only select patients you have treated experiencing inadequate pain-relief?' Eamon asked. 'There have been no other cases outside these.'

She chewed at her lip again. 'I don't know.'

'Is there anyone who you suspect who could be using you as a shield?' he asked after another pause.

She frowned at him. 'What…you mean like forging my signature or something?'

'It could be done, Erin. You don't have a particularly complicated signature. I could do it myself at a pinch.'

Her eyes moved away from his. 'I'm not sure. Why would someone do that?'

He let another silence pass, watching as she shifted her weight from foot to foot as her hands fidgeted in front of her body.

'Erin.' He drew her gaze and then locked down on it with his. 'Why didn't you have any narcotics in your trauma kit?'

Her eyes widened and her face blanched. 'Wh-what are you suggesting?'

Eamon tightened his resolve. *Keep it professional. Forget the personal. This is about patient care.* 'It is your responsibility to make sure your kit is fully stocked. You know the protocol—you sign for the drugs at the pharmacy, documentation is kept on all that are issued and all that are handed in past their due-by date.' He waited a beat before adding, 'It can all be checked by a simple phone call.'

Her body stiffened. 'You think *I* am taking drugs from the department? You think I am using drugs from my *own* bag?'

He folded his arms across his chest. 'You tell me.'

She blew out a forceful whoosh of air. 'I can't believe you would think that. What sort of person do you think I am?'

'Dr Taylor, these are very serious accusations that I—'

'So it's back to Dr Taylor, now, is it?' she asked with a flash of her toffee-brown eyes. 'That's quite a change from last night, isn't it?'

Eamon drew in a calming breath. 'I have to investigate this situation without allowing my personal feelings to get involved. I'm sorry, but that's just the way it is.'

She set her mouth. 'I quite understand, Dr Chapman. But let me assure you I am not stealing drugs from the department. The drugs from my trauma bag were stolen.'

Eamon kept his eyes trained on hers. 'Did you report it?'

She dropped her gaze, and he felt an arrow pierce his heart. 'No.'

He tightened his folded arms but the pain in his chest didn't lessen. 'Why not?' he asked. 'It's a reportable offence, Dr Taylor. Those are restricted drugs. If they are in the hands of someone who doesn't have the authority to use them, who knows what could happen. If someone dies you could be held responsible.'

She brought her gaze back to his, flashing with defiance. 'I didn't report it because…because I knew who took them.'

'Are you going to tell me who that was?'

Her mouth tightened like a knot in a piece of string. 'No, I am not.'

Anger filled Eamon's body at her intractable expression. 'Then I am afraid I am going to have to suspend your contract until this is cleared up,' he said.

Her eyes flared in outrage. 'You're firing me?'

He kept his gaze hard on hers. 'You heard me, Dr Taylor. I cannot have someone working in my department with the suspicion of drug use hanging over them. Your contract is suspended until such time as you feel able to explain to me where the missing drugs are.'

She pulled her slim shoulders back, her eyes shooting daggers of hatred at him. 'You don't have to suspend my contract, Dr Chapman.' She all but spat the words at him. 'I am resigning as of this very minute.'

Eamon watched as she spun on her heel and stalked out of his office, the door slamming in her wake, making the qualification certificates he'd only just hung on the wall rattle in their frames.

He raked a hand through his hair, a deep, ragged sigh deflating his chest. In spite of her reaction he made a

vow to himself he would do everything in his power to
clear her name. She couldn't possibly be responsible.
He knew it in his gut. She was a perfect foil for such a
scam—already known for being difficult and touchy,
she would be an easy target to lay the blame on. No one
would question it. Her career would be ruined while the
real culprit escaped the hand of the law.

At least he would be able to see her away from the
hospital—perhaps then she would open up to him, trust
him enough to tell him who she was protecting. Who
could it be? She lived alone, she didn't socialise and
she'd never had a serious boyfriend.

His stomach clenched as he thought of the intimacy
they had shared the night before. He let out another
rough-around-the-edges sigh. He only hoped she would
come to see he had no choice but to suspend her over
the allegations. Otherwise the first relationship he had
considered to be one he wanted to last for ever was
going to be over before it had a chance to begin.

As much as it pained her to do it, Erin booked Molly
into a pet boarding centre so she could escape for a few
days. The thought of running into Eamon in the lift or
in the street was unbearable. She couldn't believe he
hadn't trusted her. Sure, perhaps she should have told
him about her mother, but she had felt it was too soon
in their relationship to reveal the still-living skeleton in
her family cupboard.

She had not long returned from dropping Molly off
at the boarding centre when the phone rang. She looked
at the receiver as if it was a bomb about to go off, but
when she picked it up it turned out to be the lesser of
two evils, for once. 'Mum,' she said, laying on the

sarcasm without restraint. 'How nice of you to call. Is this call to apologise for raiding my doctor's bag, or is this a request for more?'

'Get over yourself, Ez,' Leah slurred. 'You weren't using them, why shouldn't I?'

'Because it's against the law,' Erin bit back. 'I could get you arrested. Do you realise that?'

'You wouldn't do that to your own mother.'

'Oh yeah? Well, what sort of mother are you?' Erin asked, as tears burned at her eyes. 'You're as high as a kite and you're drunk. And I lost my job because of you.'

'Told you not to sleep with the boss,' Leah said.

Erin gritted her teeth. 'What do you want?'

'I want to stay at your place for a few nights.'

'No. Absolutely not.'

'You don't mean that,' Leah said.

'Yes, I do.'

'But where will I go?'

'How about rehab?' Erin suggested coolly.

'Rehab sucks.'

'So does being stoned and drunk when you're forty-seven years old.'

'I'm your mother, Erin. You should respect me. I gave birth to you, didn't I?'

Erin felt like screaming. It was as if every childhood hurt and disappointment had gathered in her chest. It felt like a pressure cooker about to explode. She loved and hated her mother at the same time. She wanted her mother to die. She wanted her mother to live. She wanted to save her mother, and yet she wanted to be relieved of the responsibility she had been carrying for so long alone. 'Mum…' Her voice came out hoarse. 'Please don't do this to me. Not now. You can't stay here. I'm going away. I'm leaving town for a few days, maybe a few weeks.'

'Then let me house-sit for you,' Leah said. 'But before you go can you stock up on some of that brandy you had in the pantry the last time I was there? It was real special. Much nicer than the stuff I usually get.'

Erin bit the inside of her mouth to control her spiralling emotions. This was too much. Why was her life so complicated? Why couldn't she have had a milk-and-cookies mum? If destiny insisted her life had to be tough, why not just an alcoholic or just a drug user for a mother, why did she have to have both? 'Mum, I don't think you heard what I said,' she said as if speaking to a particularly inattentive child. 'I am going away and I might not be coming back.'

There was a long silence broken only by the sound of Leah sipping something from a bottle.

Erin closed her eyes against the stinging tears. 'Mum?'

'Can you lend me the money for my fare back to Adelaide, then?' Leah asked. 'I'll pay you back as soon as I get back on my feet.'

Erin let out a sigh that shredded her chest. 'I'll transfer the funds right now.'

'Thanks, Ez. I knew I could rely on you. You're the best daughter a mother could have.'

Long after her mother had hung up, Erin held the receiver against her cheek. The cold, hard phone was no substitute for the loving touch of a mother but for now, as always, it would have to do.

CHAPTER TWELVE

ERIN spent two weeks at a cottage on the Central Coast. She missed Molly dreadfully and she missed Eamon even more. She walked for miles each day, no matter what the weather dished up, trying to restore some peace to her troubled mind. She turned her phone off and resisted every temptation to switch it on to see if Eamon had tried to call her. Every way she looked at the situation, she began to see the difficult situation he'd been in as unit director. If she had told him of her worries over the second pethidine shot in the beginning, perhaps he might not have been so hasty in suspecting her. And of course if she had trusted him enough to tell him about her mother he would have seen what an impossible situation she was in. Her pride had ruined everything, just as it always had.

Maybe her mother was right: she needed to get over herself. Running away wasn't going to achieve anything. She had been running away all her life, and look where it had ended up. It was time to face things like the professional adult she had worked so hard to become. Someone was trying to sully her name and reputation and she was hiding away up here, letting them get away with it. No wonder Eamon thought she was guilty. She was acting it, and had done so from the outset.

Erin quickly packed her bags, paid her bill, left the cottage and was home with Molly within the space of a couple of hours. She went out on the balcony but her heart sank like an anchor when she saw Eamon's flat was empty. The furniture was gone, everything no doubt shifted to his newly renovated house at Balmoral Beach. She bit down on her lip until she tasted blood, the thought of having to meet him at the hospital with all those accusatory stares and whispers taking all the courage she could muster.

Somehow she managed it. She held her head high and walked through the hospital entrance and down the corridor past a couple of nurses who turned their heads as she went past to Eamon's office. It was only as she raised her hand to knock that she realised she should have phoned first.

The door suddenly opened and Eamon almost knocked her over. 'Erin!' He grasped her by the upper arms to steady her. 'Where have you been? I've been calling you for the last two weeks. Why haven't you had your phone on? I've been out of my mind with worry about you.'

Erin blinked back tears. 'I had to see you.'

He pushed open his office door and led her inside, closing it firmly behind him. 'Sweetheart, can you forgive me for how I handled things? Pulling rank on you like that.' He scraped a hand through his hair. 'God, what a jerk I've been. I should have been concentrating on getting to the bottom of this, not pointing the finger at you.'

Erin blinked at him in surprise. 'You don't suspect me any more?'

'I didn't suspect you at all, not really. I just wanted you to tell me your side, but you refused to do so. I felt I had to take a stand before things got out of hand. You know what hospitals are like. Your career would be over if word got out about this.'

She frowned at him. 'You mean it hasn't already been ruined? It's been two weeks. Surely everyone's been talking about me by now, especially with me leaving like I did?'

'Erin, I did what I could in terms of damage control,' he said. 'I had a word with the CEO and somehow managed to get Arthur Gourlay off his high horse. I pointed out to him how he could find himself with a slander case on his hands if some other explanation came to hand. The staff have been told you took some much-needed leave. You had a month owing to you in any case.'

Erin was overcome with emotion. 'I should have told you right from the start. I feel so stupid now. I should have trusted you.'

'Trusted me with what?' he asked.

She looked down at her hands clutching the strap of her handbag. 'My mother is a drug addict,' she said. She lifted her gaze back to his and continued, 'All my life I've been covering for her drug and alcohol problems. I've spent more time in foster care than with her, but she's my mum and I love her. She's not ever going to be shortlisted for Mother of the Year or anything, but she's had a tough life and I can't give up on her.'

'Oh, baby.' That was all he said. Two little words, softly delivered, but they contained a wealth of support and understanding.

Erin dropped her bag and stepped into his out-stretched arms, the feel of those strong, protective limbs coming around her making her feel as if she had finally come home. 'I should have told you. I was just so embarrassed. I can't remember a time when I haven't been embarrassed by her. I feel guilty about it. Perhaps if I was a better daughter...'

Eamon cupped her face in his hands. 'Don't blame yourself, sweetheart,' he said. 'You're a wonderful daughter. It's about her issues, not yours. Has she ever told you why it all started? Why she began drinking and doing drugs?'

Erin looked into his sea-green eyes. It felt so good to have someone to lean on for once, someone to listen to the pain of her childhood without judging. 'I think I might have told you earlier, she got pregnant with me while she was still at school. I realise it must have been tough for her. She came from a strict, conservative family. My grandparents kicked her out of their home, but I'm not sure if it was because she was sleeping around or pregnant or because of the drugs. I suspect all three.'

'Was she using before she got pregnant?'

'She was using before and during pregnancy. I was born addicted to heroin. I was in Intensive Care for three weeks. Apparently I almost didn't make it.'

His thumbs stroked her tear-stained cheeks. 'Darling girl, you really didn't get the best start in life, did you?'

She gave him a wry look. 'It gets worse.' She took a little breath and told him of the repeated stints in and out of foster care, the unsavoury boyfriends her mother had surrounded herself with, the dealers, the addicts, the drunks and the violence. Even as she told him she wondered yet again how she had survived it.

'You're an amazing person, Erin,' he said, his voice

warm and full of admiration. 'You've had so much thrown at you and yet you've risen above it. You're a brilliant doctor; you've devoted your whole life to helping people. So many others would have gone the other way, following the bad example set by their parents, but you broke the cycle.'

Erin felt comforted by his words. It helped her to finally accept what she could change and what she couldn't. 'I haven't quite given up all hope for my mother,' she said. 'I would like to think that one day she'll be able to get her life in some sort of order. It's just so hard doing it all alone. She's like a child. I feel like I've been the parent all along.'

'In many ways you have,' he said, taking her hands in his. 'Is that why you are so against having children?'

She looked into his eyes for a long moment. 'Yes and no.' She sighed again and looked back down at their joined hands, her fingers so small encased in his. 'I guess I was scared about her influence on any children I might have. What if her addiction is genetic? It's also one of the reasons I haven't dated. How do you explain to the person you've just met that your mother's a drug addict?'

He gave her hands a squeeze. 'No one should judge you for what your mother does. I certainly don't.'

'Thank you for saying that,' Erin said. 'I can't tell you how much it means to me.'

'Erin, darling.' His forehead creased in a frown. 'Does anyone at the hospital know about your mother's issues?'

She shook her head. 'No, I've never told anyone. You're the first person I've ever trusted enough to tell.'

He placed his hands on the tops of her shoulders. 'I'm going to get to the bottom of this drug thing, Erin. You have my word on that. I've been thinking it over, going through every possible scenario. But first I want your permission to have your signature analysed.'

Erin frowned. 'You mean by a forgery expert or something?'

He nodded. 'I have a mate in the police force. He specialises in this sort of thing. It's a pretty exact science. He'll be able to tell if it was you that signed for that second shot of pethidine or someone else.'

Erin was still having trouble realising he believed her to be innocent, but the more she thought about it the more it looked like she had been deliberately targeted. But who hated her that much? She knew she wasn't best friends with everyone on staff, but surely no one would set out to deliberately sabotage her career? She said as much to Eamon, but he reassured her again that he wasn't going to rest until he had cleared her name. He had already tried so hard to keep her name from being dragged down. Why had she run off without speaking to him first? She should have known he would handle the situation with the professionalism she had come to admire in him.

'Go home and rest,' he said. 'I'll drop by later tonight and take you out to dinner. I want to show you my new place. I moved in a couple of days ago.'

'I felt so disappointed when I came home to find your place empty,' she said. 'It's not going to be the same without you there.'

He kissed her in the middle of her forehead. 'There's one way to fix that, you know.'

She looked at him quizzically. 'How?'

He kissed her on the mouth this time. 'I'll tell you later.'

A couple of hours after Erin had left, Eamon looked back through the stack of patients' notes yet again. He had already faxed through the information for his friend in the police force and now wanted to check and double-check in case he had overlooked anything. It was nearly seven o'clock, and Erin would be expecting him to pick her up, but he just couldn't rest until he was absolutely certain he hadn't missed anything.

And then he found it.

It was so obvious a ten-year-old child could have solved it. He could have kicked himself for missing it. Two whole weeks had passed, and he should have picked up on it on day one when he'd first gone through the files.

How could Erin have signed for pethidine on a day she hadn't even been on duty?

His mobile buzzed on his desk and he picked it up to answer it. 'Eamon Chapman.'

'Eamon, it's Matt. I've done that analysis for you. Your girl is all in the clear. Someone's been forging her signature.'

'Yeah, I know,' Eamon said, clicking his pen on and off. 'Now all I have to do is find the real culprit.'

'Our people will have a look through the CCTV tapes,' Matt said. 'It might take a few days but something should come up.'

It had better, Eamon thought as he ended the call. Otherwise he hadn't got a hope of keeping this thing quiet for too much longer. If word started to spread, it would be like wildfire and Erin, although innocent, could get seriously burnt. Her career could be totally ruined by this type of allegation. If someone wanted to destroy her, they couldn't have thought of a better way to do it. The only question that begged to be asked was who hated her *that* much?

There was a knock on the door and he sighed as he

closed the documents in front of him. It was probably Rob Craig, the CEO. No doubt he had heard something in the loop and was coming to warn him the news was about to break in spite of his best efforts to keep things quiet.

But to Eamon's surprise it wasn't the CEO who came in and nervously took the seat opposite his desk.

'Dr Chapman? I'm sorry to disturb you, but there's something you should know about the question over pain management…'

Erin was trying to cajole Molly into forgiving her for sending her to cat crèche, but to no avail. Molly pointedly ignored the treat Erin hovered under her uptilted nose, her whiskers twitching in affront.

The doorbell rang and she left the treat on the carpet next to Molly and went to answer the door.

Eamon was standing there with a huge bunch of red roses. 'Hey, gorgeous,' he said, swooping down to plant a lingering kiss on her mouth. 'How's my girl?'

Erin could feel herself glowing at being 'his girl'. It made her feel secure in a way she had never felt before. 'I'm fine,' she said, feeling a shy blush steal over her cheeks.

He brushed one of her cheeks with his fingertips. 'God, I love it when you do that,' he said. 'It's so adorably sweet.'

Erin placed her hand over his and held it against her face. 'It's so good to see you.'

He turned over her hand and pressed a gentle kiss to the middle of her palm. 'It's good to see you too, sweetheart.' He put the roses down and pulled her into his arms, kissing her until she was breathless.

'Wow,' she said as she leaned back in his arms. 'That was certainly worth waiting for.'

'Erin.' His hands slid down her arms and encircled her wrists as if he was physically warning her that what he was about to say would be painful to hear. 'I got word back from my mate in the police force.'

She felt her breath screech to a halt. 'And?'

He gave a heavy sigh. 'Someone has been forging your signature. Just a couple of times, but it's a serious offence, given the circumstances.'

Her stomach felt queasy as she saw the gravity of his expression. 'You know who it is, don't you?'

He gave a single nod. 'I went through every roster, hoping I would find something to narrow it down, and then I saw it. I don't know why I didn't pick up on it the first time I looked. You know when you abruptly changed to night duty?'

She nodded.

'Well, that first day—in the morning, actually—your signature was on a patient's file for pethidine. But you weren't at work that day. I went through the duty roster and finally it came to me. I was about to confront the person when they came to me and confessed. That's why I was late. She came to my office just as I was leaving.'

Erin's heart gave a little lurch. 'She?'

'Lydia Hislop,' he said.

She swallowed tightly. 'Lydia?' She swallowed again. '*Lydia?*'

'I'm sorry, Erin, I know you are fond of her. And she's a damn fine nurse. But it seems she didn't do it to bring any disrepute on you. Your signature was the only person's she felt she could successfully imitate.'

'But why?' Erin asked in a cracked voice. 'Is she using? She doesn't seem the type. She's so competent. I've never seen her miss a step. Not once.'

'They weren't for her,' Eamon said soberly. 'Her mother has MS. She's in the advanced stages of the disease. Her mother made Lydia promise to assist her suicide. Lydia has been stockpiling vials of pethidine. She's been very careful, and may well have got away with it if Arthur Gourlay hadn't made such a fuss over the patients who came in under him.'

'But I saw her give Mr Yates an injection.' Erin was still trying to get her head around it all. 'I was there. I saw her administer it.'

'She swapped the vial with saline,' Eamon said. 'She felt terrible about Mr Yates almost dying. She never intended something like that to happen. She tried to select patients who would not be adversely affected, but in this case she got it horribly wrong.'

Erin felt ill. *Lydia*. Of all people! It was so hard to believe, and yet was it? Lydia was a compassionate nurse. Perhaps watching her mother's agonising decline had tipped her over. The emotional ties had blurred her judgement. How tragic that she had felt that was her only option to ease her mother's suffering. 'What will happen to her?' she asked.

'It will now become a police matter,' Eamon said. 'Lydia at least had the courage to come forward. She said she heard a couple of nurses talking about you in the rest-rooms this afternoon. They apparently saw you heading towards my office and thought you must have been called in over it. Some rumours must have already been circulating. She didn't want you to get the blame. It's sad, but that's the law. She will be prosecuted, but who knows? The courts may take into account her mother's plight. The irony is in some countries assisted suicide is legal.'

'Poor Lydia,' Erin said. 'I feel so sorry for her. I

wish I'd known about her mother. I wish I'd been more supportive.'

'Erin, you're not responsible for everyone you work with,' he said. 'But then maybe that's what I love about you—the way you try to hide how much you care. You pretend to hold people at arm's length when deep down you're just as compassionate, if not more so, than anyone else.'

Erin blinked at him and then blinked again. Had she heard him correctly? No, of course not. She was imagining it. She had to be. She had heard what she wanted to hear. She longed to hear he felt something for her, but how could he? They had only known each other such a short time.

'Aren't you going to say anything?' he asked.

She snagged her bottom lip with her teeth. 'Um…I'm not sure what I'm meant to say.'

'Did you even hear what I said?'

'What did you say?'

'I love you.'

Erin stared at him, her mouth falling open. 'I thought I'd imagined it.'

He stroked her cheek with his thumb, his eyes meltingly soft as they held hers. 'You didn't.'

Erin was still lost for words. She just stood there, looking into his eyes, wondering if she was dreaming. He loved her. For all her faults, all her insecurities, in spite of her difficult background, he loved her.

She didn't hesitate to reciprocate. 'I love you, too.'

His eyes twinkled. 'Well, that's a very fine start. When did you decide that?'

She smiled back at him. 'I think it happened the very first moment I met you. I didn't believe in love at first sight. I didn't even really believe in love, period. But now I believe it all. I *want* it all.'

Eamon's thumb stopped moving mid-stroke. 'You mean if I were to ask you to marry me and have my babies, even though we've only known each other a ridiculously short time, there's a remote possibility you might say yes?'

Erin felt her smile widen. 'I guess you'll have to ask me to find out.'

He got down on one bended knee and took both of her hands in his. 'Erin Taylor, will you marry me?'

Erin felt her heart swell to three times its size. 'Yes. Yes *Yes!*'

He rose and pulled her to her feet, wrapping his arms around her, holding her against him as if she was the most precious thing on earth. 'What changed your mind?' he asked.

She looked up into his eyes again. 'You. Your parents. Your sisters. Your little niece. You most of all. Just you.'

He kissed her tenderly, lingering over her mouth as if he never wanted to let her go. 'My beautiful, brave little Erin,' he said. 'I can't wait until you're wearing my ring and carrying my child.'

'Me too.' Erin wrapped her arms around his waist, her face pressed against the fortress-like wall of his chest. She felt safe for the first time in her life, safe and loved and protected.

And happy.

Blissfully, deliriously happy.

Her life might not have been easy, and the struggles with her mother were certainly not over yet, but somehow Erin knew that with Eamon's strong support and unwavering love they would make it.

And they did.

0310 Gen Std HB

ROMANCE

The Italian Duke's Virgin Mistress	Penny Jordan
The Billionaire's Housekeeper Mistress	Emma Darcy
Brooding Billionaire, Impoverished Princess	Robyn Donald
The Greek Tycoon's Achilles Heel	Lucy Gordon
Ruthless Russian, Lost Innocence	Chantelle Shaw
Tamed: The Barbarian King	Jennie Lucas
Master of the Desert	Susan Stephens
Italian Marriage: In Name Only	Kathryn Ross
One-Night Pregnancy	Lindsay Armstrong
Her Secret, His Love-Child	Tina Duncan
Accidentally the Sheikh's Wife	Barbara McMahon
Marrying the Scarred Sheikh	Barbara McMahon
Tough to Tame	Diana Palmer
Her Lone Cowboy	Donna Alward
Millionaire Dad's SOS	Ally Blake
One Small Miracle	Melissa James
Emergency Doctor and Cinderella	Melanie Milburne
City Surgeon, Small Town Miracle	Marion Lennox

HISTORICAL

Practical Widow to Passionate Mistress	Louise Allen
Major Westhaven's Unwilling Ward	Emily Bascom
Her Banished Lord	Carol Townend

MEDICAL™

The Nurse's Brooding Boss	Laura Iding
Bachelor Dad, Girl Next Door	Sharon Archer
A Baby for the Flying Doctor	Lucy Clark
Nurse, Nanny...Bride!	Alison Roberts

MILLS & BOON

APRIL 2010 LARGE PRINT TITLES

ROMANCE

The Billionaire's Bride of Innocence	Miranda Lee
Dante: Claiming His Secret Love-Child	Sandra Marton
The Sheikh's Impatient Virgin	Kim Lawrence
His Forbidden Passion	Anne Mather
And the Bride Wore Red	Lucy Gordon
Her Desert Dream	Liz Fielding
Their Christmas Family Miracle	Caroline Anderson
Snowbound Bride-to-Be	Cara Colter

HISTORICAL

Compromised Miss	Anne O'Brien
The Wayward Governess	Joanna Fulford
Runaway Lady, Conquering Lord	Carol Townend

MEDICAL™

Italian Doctor, Dream Proposal	Margaret McDonagh
Wanted: A Father for her Twins	Emily Forbes
Bride on the Children's Ward	Lucy Clark
Marriage Reunited: Baby on the Way	Sharon Archer
The Rebel of Penhally Bay	Caroline Anderson
Marrying the Playboy Doctor	Laura Iding

MILLS & BOON

MAY 2010 HARDBACK TITLES

ROMANCE

Virgin on Her Wedding Night	Lynne Graham
Blackwolf's Redemption	Sandra Marton
The Shy Bride	Lucy Monroe
Penniless and Purchased	Julia James
Powerful Boss, Prim Miss Jones	Cathy Williams
Forbidden: The Sheikh's Virgin	Trish Morey
Secretary by Day, Mistress by Night	Maggie Cox
Greek Tycoon, Wayward Wife	Sabrina Philips
The French Aristocrat's Baby	Christina Hollis
Majesty, Mistress...Missing Heir	Caitlin Crews
Beauty and the Reclusive Prince	Raye Morgan
Executive: Expecting Tiny Twins	Barbara Hannay
A Wedding at Leopard Tree Lodge	Liz Fielding
Three Times A Bridesmaid...	Nicola Marsh
The No. 1 Sheriff in Texas	Patricia Thayer
The Cattleman, The Baby and Me	Michelle Douglas
The Surgeon's Miracle	Caroline Anderson
Dr Di Angelo's Baby Bombshell	Janice Lynn

HISTORICAL

The Earl's Runaway Bride	Sarah Mallory
The Wayward Debutante	Sarah Elliott
The Laird's Captive Wife	Joanna Fulford

MEDICAL™

Newborn Needs a Dad	Dianne Drake
His Motherless Little Twins	Dianne Drake
Wedding Bells for the Village Nurse	Abigail Gordon
Her Long-Lost Husband	Josie Metcalfe

0410 Gen Std LP

MILLS & BOON®

MAY 2010 LARGE PRINT TITLES

ROMANCE

Ruthless Magnate, Convenient Wife	Lynne Graham
The Prince's Chambermaid	Sharon Kendrick
The Virgin and His Majesty	Robyn Donald
Innocent Secretary...Accidentally Pregnant	Carol Marinelli
The Girl from Honeysuckle Farm	Jessica Steele
One Dance with the Cowboy	Donna Alward
The Daredevil Tycoon	Barbara McMahon
Hired: Sassy Assistant	Nina Harrington

HISTORICAL

Tall, Dark and Disreputable	Deb Marlowe
The Mistress of Hanover Square	Anne Herries
The Accidental Countess	Michelle Willingham

MEDICAL™

Country Midwife, Christmas Bride	Abigail Gordon
Greek Doctor: One Magical Christmas	Meredith Webber
Her Baby Out of the Blue	Alison Roberts
A Doctor, A Nurse: A Christmas Baby	Amy Andrews
Spanish Doctor, Pregnant Midwife	Anne Fraser
Expecting a Christmas Miracle	Laura Iding

millsandboon.co.uk Community

Join Us!

The Community is the perfect place to meet and chat to kindred spirits who love books and reading as much as you do, but it's also the place to:

- **Get the inside scoop from authors about their latest books**
- **Learn how to write a romance book with advice from our editors**
- **Help us to continue publishing the best in women's fiction**
- **Share your thoughts on the books we publish**
- **Befriend other users**

Forums: Interact with each other as well as authors, editors and a whole host of other users worldwide.

Blogs: Every registered community member has their own blog to tell the world what they're up to and what's on their mind.

Book Challenge: We're aiming to read 5,000 books and have joined forces with The Reading Agency in our inaugural Book Challenge.

Profile Page: Showcase yourself and keep a record of your recent community activity.

Social Networking: We've added buttons at the end of every post to share via digg, Facebook, Google, Yahoo, technorati and de.licio.us.

www.millsandboon.co.uk